THE GOD WHO SERIES

Who Stirs Up the Sea

Deborah Raney

RANEY DAY PRESS

Who Stirs Up the Sea

Who Stirs Up the Sea is the second book in **The God Who** series by Deborah Raney.

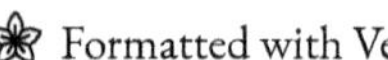 Formatted with Vellum

Other books in
The God Who series
by Deborah Raney

Who Touches the Mountains (Fall 2024)
Who Stirs Up the Sea (Summer 2025)
Who Names the Stars (Fall 2026)
Who Measures the Oceans (Summer 2027)

For I am the Lord your God,
who stirs up the sea so that its waves roar—
the Lord Almighty is his name.
I have put my words in your mouth
and covered you with the shadow of my hand...

Isaiah 51:15-16
New International Version

This is what the Lord says,
he who appoints the sun
to shine by day,
who decrees the moon and stars
to shine by night,
who stirs up the sea
so that its waves roar—
the Lord Almighty is his name...

Jeremiah 31:35
New International Version

Chapter One

April

Saint Simons Island

Emma Fiori opened the trunk of her Chevy Malibu and started loading glass vases and jars into the dusty space. Other vendors walked by carting their wares in wagons and totes, waving farewells, and looking as bedraggled as she felt.

It hadn't been her best day for sales, but at least she'd made enough to cover the rent for her space—unlike last week when she'd spent the entire day at the farmers market and ended up with a $20 *deficit* to show for her time. And even though she'd cleared a decent profit today, her proceeds barely made a dent in the payment on her car, never mind the vehicle was already ten years old and would probably conk out before she got it paid off. Plus, she was still trying to regroup from last month when she'd had to pay income taxes for the first time in her life. She started to slam the trunk lid when she caught movement from the corner of her eye.

"Hey! Flower lady! Wait up!" An athletic looking guy raced toward her waving his arms.

Slightly alarmed, she picked up an empty cardboard box and held it in front of her like a shield. As if that would offer any protection if he meant to do her harm.

But when he halted in front of her, slightly out of breath, he pointed to the jumble of bouquets in the box she'd just deposited in the back of her vehicle. "Is it too late to grab some flowers? Are those spoken for?"

"Oh... Sure. What do you want? I've got some nice tulips, or if you prefer something more formal, I have these azaleas." She lifted two glass jars of the ruffly flowers and held them out for him to inspect.

He looked between the peach and hot pink offerings.

"I could even mix these together if you want something bigger." To demonstrate, she set the jars on the pavement and pulled both bunches from the water, quickly combining the two, holding them in front of her like a bridal bouquet. The result was surprisingly stunning. "Something like this? I'll even give you a discount, say $35 for the whole bunch? Jar included."

He laughed. "Well, if you're going to include that mayonnaise jar, how could I possibly say no?"

"Exactly." Curbing a smile, she tidied a few stray blossoms and stuffed the double bouquet into one of the clear jars. "That'll be thirty-five dollars. And for the record, it's a *pickle* jar. Kosher dill, to be precise."

"Pickle? Well, in that case"—he fished in his pocket and handed her two twenty-dollar bills—"keep the change."

"Hey, thanks." She tucked the bills in her back jeans pocket. "I hope your girlfriend likes them."

He gave her a look that said *How do you know I have a girlfriend?*

"Sorry. I just assumed they're for a girl."

His smile challenged her. "How do you know they're not for my grandma?"

She shot him a dubious look. "Come on... Forty dollars? Chasing me down after the market's closed?"

He had the decency to blush. "Okay. Yeah, they're for a girl. Just a date though. Not a girlfriend."

"Well, maybe she will be after you give her these gorgeous flowers."

He shrugged. "Not really the goal, but thanks." He gave a little wave and started across the parking lot.

For some crazy reason his answer made her happy, and it wasn't just because he was cute. She turned back to the task at hand, dumping the water from the second pickle jar at the base of a palm tree and nestling the empty jar between two small jars of tulips. She should have lowered those to half price the last hour. No doubt they would have sold at five dollars each. But they would look cheery on the dining tables at Shady Acres, so it wasn't as if they were going to waste.

"You here every week?"

She started, unaware her customer had returned. He stood there, pickle jar in hand, watching her load the trunk. He appeared to be about her age, muscular and already tan, his curly brown hair lightened by the sun. He looked like he should have a surfboard under one arm.

"I'm here every Saturday. At least I try to be. Why?" She grinned. "You have a hot date next week too?"

"No, actually, I thought I'd buy some flowers for my grandma next week."

"Make an honest man of yourself, huh?" His answer made her even happier, but she shot him a suspicious grin. "Wait... Do you even *have* a grandmother?"

"I have two. But unless you ship to Cincinnati—for free— Nana's going to have to settle for a postcard."

"When will you see your other grandmother?"

"Um... Probably after church tomorrow. Why?"

Emma grabbed the jars of tulips. "Give her these. It'll save me a trip to the nursing home."

"Nursing home?"

"I usually donate anything that doesn't sell," she explained. "It makes them happy."

"Ah. Well, if you're sure. She'll like that."

She started to hand him the two jars, then realized it might be a precarious walk to his vehicle added to the larger jar. "Here, let me combine these, too." She mixed the two bouquets in one jar and handed it to him.

He held it out, turning the jar full-circle. "That's really pretty. She'll love it. Um...who should I tell her designed this arrangement?"

"Oh, that's me. Emma's Blooms." She grabbed her bank bag, unzipped it, and handed him one of her business cards.

He studied the colorful card, then looked at her. "You're Emma?"

"That's me."

"So, you *grew* these?"

She nodded, offering a guarded smile.

"Nice." He adjusted the jars, gripping the lip of one in each hand. "Well, thanks... Emma."

She watched him leave then closed the trunk. Good. That was one less trip she'd have to make on the way home. She had plenty to do before book club at her house tonight in—she checked her phone—yikes! Two hours. She needed to hustle.

Once home she started the dishwasher and quickly tidied the living room. Not that it ever got that messy with just her living here. Although she occasionally came home to a vase that Bud had knocked over, or worse, a dead mouse on the welcome mat. Of course, that was the reason she'd adopted Bud in the first place. The smoky gray tomcat earned his keep making sure the house stayed mouse-free.

As if her thoughts summoned him, the cat sauntered into the room, tail high, his gold eyes bright with mischief.

"You behave tonight, kitty-cat." She pointed at him. "You hear me?"

Bud gave his familiar chirpy meow in reply.

She'd hosted book club here once before and everyone had loved on Bud. No, more like Bud had loved on everyone. But two new members had joined since then, and she couldn't remember if she'd warned them about having a cat. She hoped nobody was allergic. Well, it was too late now.

Thank goodness, Mindy had offered to bring the snacks tonight, so all Emma really had to do once she got out of the shower was light some candles, make iced tea, and brew a pot of coffee. Mindy was providing the entertainment as well. As founder of the book club, she kept things interesting, always coming up with an activity related to the theme of whatever book they were reading. This month's suspense novel featured a DNA result that ultimately solved the crime, and since Mindy's brother worked in some kind of genetic testing lab, they'd used that company's swab kits for all the members to send off for their ancestry profiles.

Hopefully nobody would get murdered over their DNA samples the way the detective had in the novel. Emma laughed at the thought. She wasn't that excited about her results since she already knew her ancestry going back at least five generations on her Italian dad's side and two or three generations on her mom's. Still, it would be fun to do the test with the whole group and compare results.

They'd become a close-knit group over the two years they'd been meeting, and Mindy Bryson had become a dear friend, despite being ten years older.

Emma started for the shower, then turned back to survey the large room, trying to see it with fresh eyes. The linen curtains were open to the backyard gardens where the canted sun showed off the space in its best light. The gardens beyond were just beginning to look full and lush and made a colorful border for the murky green and brown salt marshes beyond.

She'd made several bouquets for the house yesterday while she arranged her vases for the farmers market, and the flowers were the finishing touch for the cozy, colorful rooms. She would set up the coffee bar later and serve snacks inside, but she hoped it would be nice enough to sit outside for their discussion. Sunsets on the island was always stunning this time of year.

Her phone rang and she ran to check it.

"Hey, Mom, what's up?" She did not have time for this.

"Oh, I just hadn't talked to you for a while and wondered what you're up to."

Guilt immediately set in. She hadn't replied to her mom's last two texts.

"I'm getting ready for book club at my house tonight."

"Oh. Well, I won't keep you then."

"I'm sorry I haven't answered your texts yet. I've been a little slammed. It's that time of year." But she had time for book club. She could almost read her mother's mind.

"It's fine, honey. It's nothing important really."

She could tell her mom was doing her best not to sound hurt, but Mom had never been great at masking her feelings. "Will you be home tomorrow morning? We can have a good talk while I weed the flowerbeds."

"You're going to weed on Sunday morning?"

"Oh, shoot! I forgot tomorrow's Sunday. What about Monday?"

"I have a hair appointment, but not till ten."

"Okay if I call you around eight then?"

"Sure, honey. That'd be fine. So, what's your big activity for book club? I know Mindy always has something fun planned."

She gave her mom an abbreviated version of the ancestry test swabs they'd done.

There was silence on the other end, and she watched the seconds tick off on her phone. "You still there, Mom?"

"Yes, I'm here."

"I thought we got cut off for a minute."

"No, I'm here. It's just... Are you sure you want your private information out there? Didn't one of those companies get hacked recently? And are those tests really that accurate? It seems like they're just kind of a gimmick."

"Oh, I think they're pretty reliable. But this is just for fun. One of the characters in our book had an ancestry test done, and Mindy's brother works for a lab that does DNA testing so she thought it would be kind of cool if we all took the test. Of course the guy in our book got killed over it."

"Oh, honey! Are you sure you should do that?"

She laughed. "It's a novel, Mom. And last I checked, I'm not related to a Mafia mob boss like that detective was." Of course, given the Fiori family's Sicilian history, she just might be, but now probably wasn't the time to bring that up.

She glanced at the clock again. "Listen, Mom, I *really* need to get in the shower. I'll talk to you Monday morning, okay?"

"Sure, sure, talk to you then."

She hung up before Mom could think of another question. But she felt awful for being so rude. Her mother was her best friend in the world, and too often lately, she'd cut conversations with her short. She set a reminder on her phone to call her first thing Monday morning, then raced for the shower.

Chapter Two

"Emma, this is absolutely charming!" Julia, one of the new book club members, stood by the living room windows, drink in hand, watching the sun slip behind the woods that edged the property, silvering the row of sweet viburnum hedges with light. "Mindy said you inherited this place? Lucky you."

Emma nodded. "It belonged to my grandparents. We're not sure when the original house was built, but Dad's parents added on sometime in the 1940s." She pointed past the hedges. "Believe it or not, where those shrubs are now used to be the front yard. But they paved over the shell roads and widened them back in the 1920s, and Nonno—my great-grandfather—decided he preferred the sunset views, so he moved the front porch to the east side where it is now and planted those hedges to hide the street. Eventually they added a patio and then covered it. Nonno and Nonni always called it the *loggia*."

Several other book club members had already taken their drinks outside. They wandered through the far end of the garden, and their exclamations over the sunset and the blossoms floated through the open windows.

Julia sighed, taking it all in. "How cool to live in a house with such history. It's just beautiful out here."

"You'll have to come back when things are really blooming."

"What do you call this?" Julia pointed to the beds of tulips and daffodils and their backdrop of blooming azalea bushes.

"That's only spring." Emma chuckled. "It'll be much more colorful a month from now. I probably spend more time on the loggia all summer than I do inside."

"I can't even imagine."

"And you said your dad's parents built this house?"

"My grandparents came over from Italy with their families when they were just teenagers. They always claimed they fell in love when they were *bambini* in Sicily." She drew quotes in the air around the Italian word. "My dad says they were probably actually in elementary school, but I love their story."

"How sweet is that?" Julia sighed before taking a long sip of her iced tea. "So you already know a lot of your ancestry. On your dad's side anyway."

"Yes, and my mom's family were from England with supposedly some Scottish ancestors way back. I guess I kind of take it for granted that I know my heritage. Do you know yours?" She guessed Scandinavian, judging by Julia's fair skin and pale blond hair.

"I know some of it. Believe it or not, my dad has some Native American blood—the Creek tribes—but mostly I'm Dutch on my mom's side."

"You must look like your mom then. It was fun doing the swabs. I never really thought about doing something like this before."

"I know. I can't wait till we get the results back and see what everybody found out. Mindy said she's already done a test."

"Yes, when her brother started working at that lab, I think. She and her brother are both adopted. I think that's how he got interested in the whole DNA thing in the first place."

"That's really cool. DNA is pretty amazing when you think about it. So, has Mindy met her birth parents?"

"It was an open adoption, so she knows her birth mother. She knows a little bit about her birth father, but he isn't in the picture."

Julia lifted a slim arm and glanced at the large face of the bracelet watch she wore. "Oh! Is this right? It's almost nine?"

Emma checked her phone and nodded.

"I'd better get home." Julia gathered her bag and books from her chair. "My mother-in-law is babysitting and I promised I'd be home in time to put the kids to bed. Let me help you clean up first though."

Emma waved her off. "No, you go on. There's not much to do. I'm just so glad you could come."

"Me too. I've really loved being in the club. It's been a good way to meet people since we moved."

"Oh, don't forget we're meeting at the library next month. Hopefully we'll have our test results back by then. Mindy said her brother was going to pull some strings and try to get them done sooner for us."

"Did I hear my name being taken in vain?" Mindy glided in from the loggia, balancing an empty teacup on its saucer.

Julia gave a little wave. "I really do need to run, but this was fun, Mindy. Great idea." She turned to Emma. "Thanks again for hosting. Your house is dreamy."

"Oh, thanks." Emma smiled, loving that adjective applied to her favorite spot on earth. "We'll be here again in September...but probably indoors unless we build a bonfire."

For September, they were reading a collection of novellas with a flower theme, and she'd agreed to host again and let everyone cut a bouquet from her garden. For their activity, she'd do a quick lesson on flower arranging for the group. Most of the weddings she'd booked would be over by then, and this would be a fun way to harvest anything still in bloom.

After Julia left, Mindy turned to Emma. "I can hardly wait for our September meeting. Your garden is already gorgeous!"

"It should be fun," Emma agreed. "If it goes well, I've actually toyed with the idea of advertising for a Girls Day Out where women could get a group of friends together, come and cut flowers, and learn some basic gardening and flower arranging tips."

Mindy frowned. "Are you sure you want to give away all your secrets? I would love that, of course, but it might be cutting off your nose to spite your face."

"Ah, you might have a point. I'll have to think that through."

Mindy took her arm and steered her to the kitchen. "You can think about it while we do the dishes."

TRAVERSING the crosswalk and dodging barricades the city had put up to temporarily close the street, Tadhg McKay spotted the dark blue Chevy Malibu in the parking lot adjacent to the farmers market and smiled to himself. He didn't know what her booth looked like but he had no trouble remembering what *she* looked like.

He turned down the first aisle and lengthened his stride—before he had time to get cold feet. Halfway down, he spotted a blue tent with the same logo from her business card, a wreath of colorful flowers and *Emma's Blooms* in a scrolly font.

She was speaking animatedly with two customers, her hazel eyes twinkling. He slowed his pace, then stopped at the booth next door to hers, pretending to be interested in a display of strong-smelling goat milk soaps. Thankfully, the vendor sitting behind the table merely said hello, then went back to the novel she was reading.

When Emma's customers wandered away, he moseyed over. Tempted to pretend he'd just happened upon her, he decided that felt disingenuous. He didn't want to start off on the wrong foot.

"Hi there."

She looked up from the bank bag she was zipping shut. "Oh, hey." Recognition lit her eyes. "How are you?"

"Good. Thought I'd just...come and see what you have for sale today."

"Ah, your girlfriend must have liked the flowers."

"It was just a date, remember? And yes, she liked the flowers. Better than she liked me, apparently." He ducked his head. Admitting he'd been dumped probably wasn't the best way to impress this woman.

Emma frowned. "Oh, ouch. I'm sorry."

He shrugged. "No biggie. It was only a second date." He was thankful now that the date had ended on a sour note.

"Still. I'm sorry."

He brightened. "But hey, Izzy—my grandma—loved her flowers. She said to tell you thank you." Izzy was actually his landlord, but she'd become like a grandma to him over the six years he'd been renting the apartment over her house.

"Oh, good. That makes me happy." Emma smiled.

She had a really pretty smile, sincere and unaffected.

Feeling awkward, but not so much that he was going to miss this opportunity, he offered a hand. "I'm Tadhg, by the way."

"Tiger?" She wrinkled her nose and the freckles sprinkled there bunched up.

"Um, Tiger minus the ER. One syllable. Tige." He repeated it, emphasizing the long *i* and the hard *g*, then rolled his eyes. "Just wait till you hear how it's spelled."

She tilted her head. "How *is* it spelled?"

"Follow along." He grinned. "T-A-D-H-G."

The freckles on the bridge of her nose bunched up further. "How do you get Tige out of *that*?"

"I know." He shrugged again, holding out his palms in surrender. "Take it up with my mom. Or probably my dad. He's the Irish one. Tadhg. To go with McKay."

She laughed. "Well, I guess I can't say much."

"Emma? Seems pretty straightforward to me."

"Yeah, but wait till you hear how it's spelled. E-M-K-Z-X-P."

"Seriously?" He cocked his head, looking doubtful.

She shot him a coy look and tucked a strand of dark blond hair behind one ear. "Just kidding."

He cracked up. "I guess I had that coming."

"Actually, it's not the Emma part that's hard. It's my last name. Fiori."

"Fiori? Sounds Italian." He rubbed thumb and fingers together and repeated her name with a thick Tony Soprano cadence.

She rolled her eyes. "Yes, but I'm *Italy* Italian, not Jersey Italian. There's a difference."

"Funny, your accent sounds pretty Southern to me, and I don't mean Southern Italy."

"And yours doesn't sound very Irish. *Or* Southern."

He affected a thick Irish brogue, which he did pretty well if he did say so himself. "Ah, but Oi can be Oirish when it suits, lass."

She laughed. "Sadly, I barely speak a word of Italian. I do know that Fiori means *flowers*." She pointed at the bouquets on the table in front of her. "Handy coincidence, huh?"

"Seriously? Your name means flowers? That's pretty cool, actually. Not that I'd want my last name to be Cable Tech. Or whatever that translates to in Irish."

"Cable Tech? That's what you do?"

He nodded. "Installation and troubleshooting." It sounded lame even to his own ears. Especially when this woman had her own business. His breath caught, and for the first time it occurred to him that there might be a Mr. Fiori. There was no diamond on her left hand, but that didn't necessarily mean anything. Maybe she took off her rings so she wouldn't lose them in all that garden dirt.

"Sounds...technical," she was saying.

"Not really." He forced himself to dial down the flirt mode. "I mean it is technical, but anybody could learn it with a little training."

"Is that what you went to school for?"

This woman was asking all the wrong questions and making him look like a total doofus. "No, it was on-the-job training. When I was in school, I actually thought I wanted to be a teacher —high school level, maybe college. Crazy, I know."

"What happened?"

"Turns out you have to get a degree to be a teacher. And it helps if you don't waste five semesters as a business major before you make that decision. I dropped out at semester my junior year." He grimaced, wanting desperately to change the subject, even while he felt relieved to get this part of his bio out of the way.

"Hey, my dad always said, 'nothing ventured, nothing gained.'"

"Yeah, I guess." That *was* good advice. In fact, he was going to take it to heart right now. "You wouldn't want to— Oh wait..." He realized he hadn't gotten the answer to his very important question. "Maybe I should ask you first: There isn't a *Mr.* Fiori, is there?"

"Two of them, actually."

"Wait. Two?"

She gave a wicked grin. "My dad and my nonno. Both in heaven now." She looked skyward.

"Oh, I'm sorry."

"No, that's good news. That they're in heaven, I mean. My dad died way too young...when I was in high school. My senior year. A car accident. And Nonno had died two years before when I was a sophomore. I miss both Mr. Fioris like crazy, but I know where they are, and I know I'll see them again."

"That's good then. Very good." It was better than good. She wasn't married and she believed in heaven. Not to mention if she turned out to be "the one" there was no father he'd have to face to ask for her hand in marriage.

"But you're not married?" Better be a hundred percent sure.

"Oh. No. Not yet."

"Not yet? Engaged?"

"Nope. Don't even have a boyfriend. Just hope to someday." She said it without a shred of embarrassment.

His sigh came out louder than he intended. "In that case, you wouldn't want to go out with me, would you?" His invitation came out way sooner than he'd intended too.

She paused. "And where are you going to buy *my* flowers from?"

He struggled for a reply until her impish grin told him she was teasing. "Oh, those don't come till the second date." Two could play this game.

She grinned.

"But don't worry," he said. "If we get that far, I know a place."

She laughed out loud, but just as swiftly, her expression turned serious. "This isn't a rebound thing is it? I mean, are you just serial dating until you find somebody who wants to go on a third date?"

He cocked his head and stared at her. "Well, I guess you could say that. Not the rebound part," he added quickly. "But what's dating for if not trying to find somebody who wants to go out with you more than once?"

"Hmm... Good point. So, where and when?"

"How about Wednesday night?"

"Ooh, sorry, I can't do Wednesday. That's when my small group from church meets."

"Oh. Next Saturday then?"

She cringed again. "I'm so sorry. I'm doing flowers for a wedding that night."

He forced a grin. "Okay, I see how this is gonna go. And I bet you're washing your hair on Friday?"

She laughed. "Well, maybe, but no, I promise it's not that. And in fact, I just happen to be free Friday night."

Now it was his turn to cringe. "Sorry, I can't on Friday."

"Okay, I see how this is gonna go." She mimicked his tone.

"No, I really do have something going on then. But what about Sunday night?"

"Bingo. I'm free."

"For bingo?"

"I was kidding, but"—she shrugged one shoulder—"if you want, sure."

"Maybe dinner and a walk on the beach instead?" Girls around here seemed to really like that walk on the beach stuff.

She grinned up at him. "Even better. It's a date."

"How about if I pick you up around five?"

"Would you mind if we meet at the restaurant?" She wrinkled her nose in that cute way of hers. "I haven't had time to do a background check on you yet."

He laughed. "I'm Irish. What more do you need?"

"Date of birth, Social Security number, school transcripts..." She counted them off on slender fingers. "Seriously though, I gave you my card, right? You can text that number about where to meet later this week."

"Deal." He already wanted a second and third date with this Emma Fiori.

$$Chapter\ Three$$

May

Emma arrived at the restaurant twenty minutes early and sat on the covered porch where she could watch for her date. She checked her phone to be sure he hadn't left a message since he'd texted to suggest they meet here at Fiddlers. It was one of her favorite restaurants on Saint Simons Island.

There was a message from Mom she'd missed, but that could wait till she got home. They'd had a good, long visit last Monday. She tucked her phone back into her crossbody bag and zipped it.

When she looked up again, Tiger stood there grinning, a canvas shopping bag lopped over one shoulder. "Hi there."

"Hi... Tiger."

"Hey, you remembered."

"Of course. Tiger without the ER though. Tige. I remember how to pronounce it, but please don't ask me to spell it. And let me confess that not knowing how to spell your name *seriously* curtailed my ability to run a background check on you."

He shot her a grin before leading the way inside the restaurant where the host led them to a booth.

He slid into the seat across from her, placing the canvas bag on the bench beside him. "That's a relief you couldn't do that background check. Tell you what, I'll friend you on Facebook."

"Not until the third date." She gave him the side eye. "Did you do a background check on *me*?"

"Just found you on Facebook. That's all. And in case you forget my name—" He pushed up the sleeve of his T-shirt to reveal an impressive prowling tiger on an equally impressive bicep. "Tiger works."

"That's cool." She wasn't usually a fan of tats—or of guys showing off their biceps—but this tattoo was a work of art and an appropriate reminder given his hard-to-pronounce name. And it wasn't like he was flexing or anything. "Did that hurt?"

"Getting inked?"

She nodded.

"A little. But that was kind of the point."

She shook her head. "I don't understand."

He waved her off. "Sorry. It's a long story. For another time maybe."

"Second date?" She wished she hadn't said that, in case tonight was a bust. But now she was curious. "So, is that what your name means? Tiger?"

"No." He chuckled. "Actually, Tadhg means storyteller. Or poet, but I couldn't rhyme if my life depended on it."

"Poems don't *have* to rhyme, you know."

"True," he conceded.

"So, *storyteller*, are you going to tell me the story?" She motioned toward his tiger tattoo, which was now hiding under his sleeve. "About why pain was the point?"

"Another day." His broad smile kept the reply from being terse. "Oh, before I forget… I brought you something." He lifted the bag and slid it across the table to her.

"For me?"

He nodded, waiting with a knowing grin. "Careful. It's breakable."

She looked inside and pulled out a large pickle jar. Not the one she'd given him. This one, though sparkling clean, still had the labels on it. "Hey, thanks. I can't eat pickles fast enough to keep me in jars."

He gestured toward the bag. "There's another one in there too. I don't know if it's big enough, but I thought it would work for flowers. In your booth, you know."

She pulled out a small bundle of newspaper and carefully unwrapped it to reveal a uniquely shaped jar. She held it up to the light. The pressed glass looked like something that might have held jam or preserves fifty years ago. "It's beautiful. I think it might be old. Where'd you get this?"

"It was in this shop in Brunswick."

"Wow. Thank you. Can I pay you for it?"

"No way. It was only a couple bucks. Probably because it has a crack in it." He pointed to a little chip on the rim of the jar.

"That's no big deal. The leaves will cover that up."

"And I had some store credit at that shop," he admitted. "Think of it as first-date flowers."

She laughed. But he'd paid a lot more than two dollars if it was the shop she was thinking of. "You said you had credit? Are you an antique-er?"

That shrug again. "I like auctions. And thrift stores. The shop takes my stuff on consignment sometimes."

"Cool. Well, thank you for this." She clutched it to her chest. "It's kind of too pretty to sell. I might just use it at home—if that's okay with you?" she added quickly.

"Of course. Suit yourself. I just thought it looked like something you could put flowers in."

"Definitely. Thank you. And for the pickle jar too."

"We can put it in your car before we go walking—so you don't have to carry it."

"Good idea."

He wrapped the smaller jar in the newspapers again before stuffing both jars back in the bag.

Their server came and took their drink orders, but by the time he returned with their iced teas, they were so deep in conversation, they'd forgotten to look at the menu. "Give us a couple of minutes, would you?" Tadhg asked.

They studied the menu in silence for a few minutes but as soon as they placed their orders, they picked up where they'd left off in their conversation. She liked this guy, and unless things went south before the night was over, she hoped he would ask her for that second date. And not just because of the flowers.

The seafood they'd both ordered was delicious, but after sharing a slice of the restaurant's signature Key Lime Pie, she was thankful they planned to walk after dinner.

They deposited the jars in her car and struck out toward the beach, taking the footpath by the marsh along Ocean Boulevard until they came to Massengale Park where there was easy beach access.

The evening was cool and as the wind picked up, Emma was glad she'd thought to bring a jacket, but their brisk pace kept them warm. And if it hadn't, their conversation would have.

They crossed the access mats and a short pontoon bridge, and when they reached the beach, they both slipped off their sandals and picked their way barefoot to the water's edge. The sand on East Beach was clean and hard-packed, and despite being cold, it felt good under her toes.

To their right, lights twinkled from the hotels, and music and laughter wafted from the resort's patios.

A group on bicycles rode past them, but when they had the beach mostly to themselves again, he turned to her.

"So, tell me about this farm of yours. Is it the family farm or do you run it yourself?"

"Just me, but it might be a stretch to call it a farm. I only have a little over an acre and that includes the house." She held up a hand. "I know my business card says *flower farm* on it, but that's just so people understand that I grow my own flowers. And for the kind of sales I do, an acre is plenty for flowers."

"I'd say that qualifies as a farm."

"Except most people think barns and horses and cows when they hear that word."

"But there are fish farms and dairy farms and funny farms..." He gave her a sideways glance.

"That's probably the most accurate description of mine. When you meet Bud, you'll see why." She wished she'd said *if you ever meet Bud*, but the truth was, she was already starting to feel hopeful about this guy.

"Bud?"

"That's my cat."

A light came to his blue-gray eyes. "Ohhh, Bud...like a flower bud. Or a bud vase."

"Oooh! Look at you...you got it. Hardly anybody ever does. His full name is Rosebud, but he decided that was kind of a wimpy name for a tomcat so we compromised with Bud."

Tadhg laughed. "He sounds like my kind of guy."

"He's great. As cats go. I grew up with dogs but before I could get a dog, I got mice, so I adopted Bud."

"And is he a mouser?"

"A very good one. At least I don't have mice in the house anymore. What about you?"

"Nope, no mice in my house either."

She gave him a playful shove with one shoulder. "I meant do you have any pets?"

"Not now. I've thought about getting a dog, but I'm too lazy and too poor. My landlady charges a hundred dollars a month extra if—"

She raised an eyebrow. "Landlady?"

"Landlord." He shrugged. "She calls herself a land*lady* though, so that's what I call her. Anyway, she charges extra if you have pets."

"Ouch."

"Yeah. So I'm dog-less for now. Maybe someday."

"So, you live on the island?"

He nodded. "I grew up in Ohio, but we vacationed here

almost every summer while I was growing up. I always knew I'd come here to live once I was on my own."

"You have brothers and sisters?"

"Two brothers. I'm an oops baby, so they're a lot older than me. Liam's"—he counted on his fingers—"thirty-eight. So Declan must be in his forties."

"Liam and Declan," she echoed. "And Tadhg. Good Irish names. So, are you close? With your brothers?"

He frowned. "We get along. But they're both married with kids, so they still think of me as the little kid I was when they left home. Never mind I'll turn thirty in September."

"Ooh, you're an old man."

"What about you?" He gave a little wince. "Or is that a rude question?"

"Not rude. I'll turn twenty-eight next month. And now you know my middle name."

"I do?"

"June." She grinned. "Emma June. E.J. until I hit the ripe old age of twenty-five and decided I liked my name after all."

"It's nice. But why twenty-five?"

"I don't know. I guess—" She'd been about to reveal more than she usually shared with a relative stranger. But then she realized she *wanted* to share with him. "I was kind of a tomboy and some people thought E.J. was a boy's name. I kind of panicked when I hit twenty-five and I still wasn't married. So I decided to capitalize on my feminine side. Obviously it didn't get me anywhere, but at least I feel like I've grown into my name now."

He glanced over at her, inspecting from head to toe—and somehow, his appraisal didn't feel the least bit inappropriate, especially when he met her gaze with an almost sympathetic smile. "Would I be out of line to say that I would never in a million years mistake you for a dude?"

"Thank you. I think." She laughed.

"I never did get why women are so touchy about telling their age. But maybe that's only if you're not married by a certain magic number?"

"Maybe. It seems kind of silly now. Twenty-five isn't old." She feigned a frown. "Now, twenty-eight is getting up there."

He scoffed. "I can't even remember back that far."

They walked in silence for a while. The light melted toward the horizon and waves came ever closer to their footprints in the sand, the water's soothing rhythm a sound that made Emma hope there were beaches in heaven.

Finally Tadhg broke the silence. "So, have you ever been serious with anyone?"

"Not really. I've dated a couple of guys—" She tossed him a mischievous sidewise glance. "—for more than three dates, I might add. But never anybody I was serious about. I'm kind of picky, I guess."

"Uh-oh. And yet you agreed to go out with me."

"I know," she teased. "What was I thinking?" But not wanting to miss her chance to get *his* answer, she asked, "What about you? I know you're a serial dater, but anybody serious?"

"Once. A long time ago. Or at least it feels like it. Becca. She broke my heart."

"Aww, I'm sorry."

"It's okay. I'm over it now. And she's happily married with two kids and another one on the way."

"Oh wow. She didn't waste any time, huh?"

"To be fair, we were college sweethearts and she was a year older than me, so she's probably right on schedule."

"Well, women have that ticking clock, you know."

"Do you?"

This was pretty tender territory for a first date, and yet, the way he asked, it felt like the most natural question in the world, and she answered in kind. "I probably do. I mean, I want kids and everything. But I just decided if it's supposed to happen it will. It doesn't pay to cry over something you don't have. And it sure doesn't pay to try to manufacture it."

"Oh. Ouch."

"What?" She looked over at him, thinking he must have stepped on a sharp shell or something.

"No. Ouch about trying to manufacture it. That hits a little too close to home."

"Sounds like there's a story there."

He pushed up his sleeve to let the tiger show. "It may or may not be related to *this* story."

"Ah. I see. For another time though?"

He nodded. "Probably best."

"Hmm... If we've already covered ticking biological clocks and old flames this must be quite the story."

He reached for her hand in a way that didn't feel forced—or even romantic, really. It felt exactly right.

"Do you want to try to find some coffee?"

"I'd like that."

"Maybe if you get me hopped up on caffeine you can pry that story out of me."

The smile he gave her kept her from being scared off by whatever dark secret he might be going to reveal. And the way he squeezed her hand made her feel like something wonderful was unfolding. Something she should try to capture in her memory forever. She was afraid to blink lest the spell be broken.

Chapter Four

Tadhg remembered seeing a sign pointing toward coffee a ways down the beach. He watched for it as they walked, suddenly nervous about his implied promise to tell what he'd come to think of as "the tiger story." He'd scared off more than one pretty girl with that tale—no pun intended—but long ago, he'd decided it was only fair to give anyone he was genuinely interested in the chance to abandon ship before things got too serious.

But he'd never met anyone like Emma Fiori—so unaffected and happy-go-lucky—and he didn't want to blow any chance he had with her before their first date was even over.

They rounded a dune and stared at the Closed sign in dismay. The coffee shop had closed at six.

"We can go back to The King and Prince," he told her. "I'm pretty sure there's a place to get coffee there. You mind walking a little more?"

"Not at all."

They retraced their steps, and a few minutes later they settled in at the island resort in comfy chairs under strings of party lights with the sky over the sea turning a dozen shades of orange and red before it faded to violet. They sipped their hot drinks in silence appreciating the night's fleeting beauty.

When the show ended and the sun had finally disappeared below the horizon, he turned to her. "So, tell me how you came to have a farm on the island."

"Well, like I said, it's not really a farm. One point three two acres, to be exact. But the property has been in my dad's family since the 1930s. My dad was an only child, so when Nonni passed away, I inherited the house."

"Does your mom live there too?"

"Oh no, Mom remarried not long after Dad died, and once I graduated high school, they moved to Bill's house in Savannah. They tried to get me to come with them, but this is home. I grew up here. Well, over in Brunswick, but we spent a lot of time at Nonni's. Even when I was young, I always knew I wanted to live in their house someday."

"That's a pretty awesome inheritance."

She nodded. "It really is. The truth is, Mom thought I should sell it—to fund my college education. But there are too many memories there. And besides, I never really had any reason to go to college. I wish I hadn't wasted two semesters there. But there's no way I could live on what I make with my business if I had to pay rent here. And of course, real estate is bonkers here."

"Tell me about it. I just rent a small apartment over a house, but even that's not cheap. There's no way I could afford a house on the island." It comforted him a little to know that she was a college dropout too. Of course she ran her own successful business. There was that.

"So, how long have you lived here?"

He thought for a minute. "Five years now, I guess...since I quit at semester my junior year at Cleveland State. That's when I saw the job at Cable Solutions advertised and applied online—from Ohio. When they called me for an in-person interview, I brought all my stuff with me, and I've been here ever since. It's home to me too now."

From the corner of his eye, he saw someone approach their table. He looked up to see a pretty blond looking hesitantly at Emma. A man hung back, wrangling two small children, waiting rather impatiently for her.

"Emma? I thought that was you."

She looked up and recognition lit her hazel eyes. "Hey, Julia. How are you?"

"Good. Sorry to bother you..." She looked pointedly at Tadhg as if waiting for an introduction.

He smiled and gave her a nod, but when Emma merely waved away the woman's apology, she spoke quickly. "I just wondered if you got your test results back yet. Mindy called to tell me, so I checked and mine is here!"

"Wow, that was fast," Emma said with a broad smile.

They must not be talking about life-and-death hospital test results.

"I know! I don't know if I can wait until our next meeting for the big reveals."

"You'd *better* wait! We agreed."

Julia laughed. "I know, I know. It'll be fun. Oh—" Julia waved her husband over. "I don't think you've ever met Jack, have you?"

"No, I don't think so." Emma scooted her chair back and offered her hand to Julia's husband. "Nice to meet you. And this must be Elliot and—" She threw Julia a look of desperation. "So sorry... I remember it starts with E, but—"

"I'm impressed you remember that. This is Eva."

"Eva. Of course." Emma bent and shook hands with each of the kids.

Tadhg warmed even more to her, watching their sweet interactions. Then she straightened and turned to him. "This is my friend, Tadhg."

She said his name as if they'd been friends all their lives, but he got the distinct impression that Emma wanted to avoid an opportunity to explain their relationship further.

He rose from his chair and shook hands with the couple. "Tadhg McKay. Nice to meet you."

Emma told her friend's husband again that it had been nice to meet him, then gave Julia a little wave. "Nice to run into you."

"You too. Well... We'd better get these kiddos home to bed. But I'll see you at book club." Julia herded the little family toward the exit.

"You too."

"Book club friend?" he asked when they were out of earshot. He took his seat again.

"Yes. Julia just started coming this year. They moved here from the west coast to be closer to his parents."

"So, they test you at this book club of yours?"

She looked askance at him.

"Your friend said your tests were back...or something like that."

"Oh, that." She laughed. "We all did ancestry tests—DNA— at our last meeting. The woman who started the book club always does something fun related to the book we read."

"Cool. I never thought about doing that just for fun...an ancestry test, I mean."

"No, me neither. Seems like you usually hear about them when somebody needs an organ donor, or their paternity is in question or something." She made a face. "The guy in our novel got whacked when they figured out his DNA."

"Wow. I hope it goes better for your club."

She laughed. "That's what my mom said. But I don't think anybody there is on a hit list, so we're probably safe."

"You said you know your grandparents' ancestry already. Both sets?"

She nodded. "My mom's parents lived in Savannah where Mom grew up."

"They don't still live there?"

"No, they passed away a few years ago."

"Oh. I'm sorry. At least they lived close when you were growing up, so you must have seen them often."

"Not really. Mom wasn't as close to her parents as Dad was to his, so we didn't see them as often. They both died during the pandemic so we didn't even have funerals for them." She'd said it almost matter-of-factly and wished she could take that attitude back.

"Oh, wow...I'm sorry. They died of Covid?"

"Yes. Complications of it anyway. Grandma fell and broke her hip, so she was already compromised. Grandpa's Covid turned into pneumonia. My mom thinks he just didn't have the will to fight it after Grandma passed away. He died ten days after she did. It was pretty brutal."

"I can't even imagine. I'm so sorry."

"Thank you. It sometimes feels weird that my mom and I are the only ones left on both sides of my family. I feel like I'm too young for that."

"For sure." He wasn't sure how to respond. He loved his family, but he'd always felt a little on the outside. It was his own fault, and not something he spent a lot of time dwelling on. By the time he turned ten, his brothers had both been off at college and they'd never really been close, especially after his brothers got married. Recently, Liam and his wife had made an effort to get back in touch, even asking if there was a good time they could come to visit. But he still hadn't gotten back to them with a date. He'd been kind of hoping they'd just forget. What on earth would they talk about?

He felt the pressure of Emma's hand on his arm. "I'm sorry. I didn't mean to be a downer."

"No...no, you weren't. I was just thinking... I probably don't appreciate my own family as much as I should." He made a mental note to call Liam this weekend.

"You said they're all back in Ohio?"

"Yes. They're still in the little town we grew up in outside of

Cincinnati. I'm sure my mom would appreciate it if I came home once in a while."

"You don't?"

"It's been a couple years." More like three and a half.

"Tadhg! But you call home every week, right?"

He shot her a look. "I bet *you* don't even call home every week."

"That's because I see my mom in person at least two or three times a month."

"Yeah, but it's not a twelve-hour drive."

"True. But a phone call doesn't take twelve hours."

"Okay, okay...I'll call my mom." He made another mental note.

"But wait...doesn't your grandma live close by?"

He squirmed and ducked his head. "I was afraid you were going to bring that up."

She waited, looking dubious and more than a little annoyed.

He struggled with how to answer, but before he could think of an explanation that wouldn't make her mad, she spoke up.

"Please don't tell me you made up that grandma. And going to see her after church?" Now she almost looked annoyed.

He held up a hand. "I do have a nana in Cincinnati. And I swear I didn't make up the grandma or the church. She's just not actually...*my* grandma."

Emma crossed her arms at her waist, studying him. "I'm listening."

"She's actually my landlord."

"You mean the land*lady*?"

"Exactly." He grinned. "Her name is Izzy. But I really do think of her as a grandma. She's the one I took the flowers to. And she did love them. I wasn't lying about that."

"But the grandma part?"

"Okay. I probably should have explained that better. I promise I wasn't trying to scam you out of flowers or anything. It was just easier and...well, back then, I didn't think I'd ever see you again." Was that true? He was on probation here and he didn't want to blow it with this woman.

"So, you only lie to strangers? Is that it?"

He couldn't tell if she was truly upset or just giving him a hard time. "No. I really don't, Emma. Calling Izzy my grandma just kind of fit into the joke we had going, if you remember. I swear I wasn't trying to pull one over on you. I was just...flirting."

"Flirting on your way to a date with another girl...*if you remember*." She mimicked him.

And it stung. "I'm sorry. I...I can guess how that must sound. Feel. Maybe there are some things I need to explain. If you even care."

"I care. I'm listening." But walls had gone up. He could see it in her eyes.

"I really didn't want to dive into this quite so soon." Boy, was that an understatement. He took a deep breath. *Lord, give me the words.*

Chapter Five

Emma shivered and shifted in her seat, a pall of gloom settling over her. She liked this guy so much. And she'd been stupid enough to think maybe something special was happening between them. That was her own fault. She'd fallen for him way too soon. Long before she had a chance to get to know who he *really* was. Why did she let herself be charmed so easily? She wasn't that desperate. Was she? Too often, the charmer turned out to be nothing on the inside like he'd sold himself to be on the outside.

But like so many other times, the warnings Tadhg had hinted at convinced her tonight would be the end of it. Like every other man she'd started to fall for, Tadhg McKay apparently had a dark secret, or a past that would simply be too hard to forgive. Or at the very least, keep her from being able to completely trust him.

He sat across from her twisting his empty coffee cup on a paper napkin until it left a round indention. He kept his head down, almost as if he was praying.

When he finally looked up, she asked quietly. "So, is this the tiger story?"

"You could say that. At least it leads to the tiger story." The smile he gave her made her feel sadder still, but he plowed ahead.

"I feel like I'm walking a tightrope here. This really isn't a first date kind of conversation, but I feel like if I don't tell you, I won't ever get a chance for a second date. I don't want you to think the worst..."

Well, he had that part right. "I'm not sure what 'the worst' even is, but...just tell me. And I'll let you know whether it's worse than the worst I'm thinking."

Her attempt at humor fell flat and he frowned. "Okay. I'm just going to put it all out on the table. I would like—someday before I'm fifty-three—to be married." He held up a hand as if anticipating an interruption.

But she stayed silent. Waiting, even as a glimmer of hope flickered.

"I only say that because I feel like you think the fact that I've dated a few girls for only two dates means I'm a player. Means I'm fickle. I'm not, Emma. But when I date someone, if I realize after a couple of dates that she's just not someone I could see as my wife — I don't want to waste my time. *Or* hers. And maybe you think if I don't ask a girl out for a third date that there needs to be some kind of— I don't know...*buffer* before I ask someone else out. But why? It's not a rebound thing. I promise. There was nothing to rebound from. But when you get to be my age—"

"Oh, you're *so* ancient." She clapped a hand over her mouth. "Sorry. Go on."

"It's just that there are a lot of women who have...a history. I don't mean to sound judgmental. It's not like I don't have a history myself. But—" He blew out a breath and gave her a look that said *Should I even bother trying to explain?*

"Go on," she said again, trying to sound empathetic. "I'm listening."

"Okay, here's the deal. I was engaged when I was twenty-four. I fell hard and life looked good, and then two weeks before our wedding day she decided she wasn't ready to be married. And by that I mean, she wasn't ready to be married to *me*. Turns out, she'd met a guy at her work. Nothing happened between them—

at least that's what she said—but the feelings she had for him made her think she wasn't ready to commit to just one person."

"Oh Tadhg. I'm sorry." That was not what she'd expected to hear.

He waved her off. "It was a long time ago. Six years now. And I guess I'm glad she decided that before we got married. But for a while it pretty much broke me. And I don't mean financially, though it didn't do me any favors in that department either. I went into kind of a depression—"

"Of course. Who wouldn't? That would be hard for anybody."

"I know. I'm not apologizing for being depressed. But I didn't handle it very well. I...started drinking. Got into a couple of bar fights. Like call-the-cops bar fights." He held up a hand. "I mean, I never killed anybody or...went to prison, but it was pretty bad. I wasn't a very nice person back then. Honestly, I'm sure it's one reason my brothers kind of backed off from me. They'd both just had their first kids, and I was not somebody they wanted their kids to grow up around. Not that I can blame them."

He raked a hand through his hair and even in the shadows cast by the party lights overhead, she could see the anguish in his expression. Her heart went out to him, and yet a caution light still blinked. She got the impression there might be even more to come.

She tried to think of something to say that would comfort him, yet not make him think she was sympathetic either. What he'd confessed made her wonder just what she was getting into. But no words came. So she waited.

Finally he sighed and the words poured out. "Everything was about Tadhg back then. I figured if Becca—that was her name—if she didn't care how bad she'd hurt me, then I had to take care of myself. Be a tough guy. Somewhere in the middle of it all, I went and got the most important thing, me, Tadhg"—he affected a swagger—"inked on my arm. And to answer your question from the other day—it hurt like the devil."

She winced involuntarily.

"And I liked that pain. Felt like I deserved it." He rolled his eyes. "I know. *Wah, wah, wah.* I finally got so stinkin' sick of me... But I couldn't get away from me." He rubbed the sleeve where the tattoo was, as if feeling the pain anew. "It's a reminder now."

"A reminder?"

"That it's *not* about me. That I am not the boss of me. He is." He pointed a finger heavenward.

Emma gave a soft smile, feeling more hopeful—and relieved— by the minute.

"I wasn't lying when I said I've always wanted to live here on the island, but I admit when I moved here, I was running away. I just didn't realize then that it was myself I was running from. Thankfully, I ran straight into a church the first week I got here. That's a whole story in itself, but bottom line? That morning Jesus Himself had a little come-to-Jesus meeting with me—" He glanced up at her with a cute smirk.

She couldn't help but smile. And not just because of his joke. She was truly happy that he'd found his answer there. And that it had apparently stuck. But she still had questions.

He touched her hand briefly across the table. "All that to say, I hope I'm not that jerk anymore. I'm not claiming to be perfect or anything, but Tadhg 2.0 is much improved—and working on version 2.1."

His touch warmed her, though no words formed in her mind. Beyond the beach below them, the sea reflected a fingernail moon, and the rhythm of the waves could just barely be heard over the music on the hotel's sound system.

After a few seconds of her silence, he spoke again. "I guess, at the risk of scaring you off, you should know that I was dead serious when I said that I want to—eventually—be married. I want a family like my brothers have. After what happened with Becca, I'm a little gun-shy. But my philosophy is if you want to get married, don't waste any time dating a girl you wouldn't want for a wife. And...well, you seemed like a possibility. Still do. So far."

He winked but quickly turned serious again. "So, yes, I was flirting with you that day. And I'm not apologizing."

"Wow. That's...a lot." It *was* a lot. So why did she feel so happy?

He gave a short laugh. "Hey, if that creeps you out a little, I totally understand."

"Tadhg... I'd like to be married too—*eventually*. And it makes sense not to waste time with someone you know doesn't want the same." And he was right that it wasn't exactly the easiest topic to broach on a first or even a second date.

He leaned closer. "I won't rush you, Emma—if you're even willing to go out with me again after hearing all that. But if you are, I promise I'll take it slow. One date at a time until one of us is sure this isn't meant to be."

She shrugged. "Or—until both of us are sure it *is*."

His smile said he liked the way she was thinking. "So, does that mean you'll go out with me again?"

"It does."

He pumped a fist in the air and mouthed an enthusiastic *Yes!*

She couldn't help but laugh.

It was late when she got home, but Emma texted her mom, hoping she was still up to talk. She didn't often talk to her about the men she dated—at least not until it got serious, which hadn't happened in a long time—but Tadhg was different. And she was too wound up to sleep. She had to tell someone.

> Emma: You still up?

> Mom: I'm awake. Bill's not home from his meeting yet. What's up?

> Emma: I met somebody. :)

Mom: Somebody as in a boy?!?!

She giggled and typed out her reply.

Emma: A MAN, actually.

Mom: I'm calling you right now.

Emma laughed out loud and waited for her phone to ring. "Hi, Mom?"

"A man? How old? We're not talking, like, somebody old enough to be your father?"

She curbed a smile. "He *is* an older man."

"Emma June? How much older?"

"Settle down, Mom. He's thirty."

A long pause. "That's pretty old. Please don't tell me you met him online."

"Mother! You do remember that I'm almost twenty-eight, right?"

"I know, but you seem so much younger. Okay, tell me all about this man child."

She laughed. "His name is Tadhg. Tadhg McKay, and I met him at the farmers mar—"

"Wait. *What's* his name?"

She gave Mom the same explanation Tadhg had given her the second time they talked. "It's Irish."

"I'm not sure how I feel about my daughter dating somebody named Tiger, but go on..."

Emma strung out the story for her mother's benefit, loving that she could hear both apprehension and guarded excitement in her voice. She and her mom had always been close, but after Dad's death, they'd truly become friends. "I really like him, Mom."

"But you've only known him for a couple of weeks, right?"

"I know, I know. I'm not in love or anything. But it's been a long time since I met anyone that even felt like a possibility."

"I'm happy for you honey. Just—please take it slow."

"Don't worry." She giggled. "Although, we did talk about marriage tonight."

"You *what?*"

"I'm just trying to get you riled up."

"You're just trying to give me a heart attack is more like it." A commotion in the background stole Mom's attention. "Honey, Bill's home. Can I call you back?"

"Oh, you don't need to. I just had to tell somebody."

"Well, I'm happy for you. Not ready to plan a wedding or anything, but very happy for you. You'll let me meet him, of course." It wasn't a question.

"If it gets serious, I promise. Tell Bill hi for me."

"I will. Love you."

"Love you too."

She clicked End and cradled the phone to her chest. She'd told her mom she wasn't in love, but she was definitely falling in that general direction.

Chapter Six

"Okay ladies, take your seats, please. Everybody listen up." Mindy waved both hands over her head, trying to get the attention of a dozen chattering book club members. They were meeting in the public library tonight so the chaos was slightly subdued, but only slightly.

With a finger to her mouth, Emma interrupted Julia mid-diatribe about her mother-in-law, then pointed to Mindy, who was still waving wildly.

When the room finally quieted, Mindy smiled conspiratorially and held up her phone with a colorful app lighting the screen. Emma recognized the logo of the ancestry sight they'd used.

"You should have all gotten your results back by now. Now just a reminder, the type of test we took isn't meant to give medical information or connect you with long lost cousins or anything like that, but according to my brother, it should show you your basic ancestry quite accurately. Okay, are we ready?" Mindy shook a finger at them. "Did anyone cheat and look at your test already?"

Nervous laughter rippled through the room. Beside Emma, Julia squirmed before raising a hand half-mast. "I confess."

"You little cheater," Emma whispered, nudging her playfully.

"I just couldn't wait to find out who I am!"

Everyone laughed, and Mindy waited for the group to quiet again. "If you don't have the app on your devices yet, there's a QR code with the link on the screen behind me."

Some of the older women shot confused looks at each other, and Emma scooted her chair forward to help Grace Simmons in the row in front of her download the app.

The room buzzed with little groups of women exclaiming over each others' results. Emma wondered if some of the women might actually be afraid of what their test might reveal. But she watched Grace beam as her results confirmed her English ancestry on both sides. "My uncle wrote our family genealogy going back to the seventeenth century in Yorkshire."

Julia showed Emma her graphs indicating that besides her Dutch and Creek Indian roots, she had a significant percentage of Scottish blood running through her veins.

"That really surprised me. But hey, aren't you going to look at yours?" Julia motioned pointedly at Emma's phone.

"Oh! Of course." She clicked on the app. "I downloaded it the night we did the swabs, but I haven't opened it since—because I was afraid I'd be tempted to cheat." Grinning, she elbowed Julia again.

"I know, I know. I should have left it alone too."

A colorful chart similar to Julia's appeared on the screen. "This blue will be my Italian side." She curved her finger around a band that represented over fifty percent of her heritage." The next largest band was yellow. "That's probably the Scottish, but I figured it'd be pretty much half and half." She enlarged the image on her screen.

Julia looked over her shoulder. "No, the blue is the Scottish part, Emma. And that yellow is European with...looks like northern Europe and a sliver of French—"

"What? Wait... Then where's the Italian?" She made the image larger still and scrolled down the page where the different statistics were given in more detail.

"I don't see any Italian." Julia frowned. "Go back up. Are you sure you didn't get somebody else's test?"

Emma scrolled to the top where her profile photo stared back at her. "It says it's me. That's weird... It should be at least fifty percent Italian, shouldn't it? My dad's parents were both *born* in Sicily—and their parents too, I think. Or at least near there. I'm Italian." The words came out more like a question.

"I'm sure it's just some sort of mix-up or...a glitch in the software or something." But it was obvious Julia was grasping at straws.

Emma excused herself and went to talk to Mindy. She had to wait for her friend to finish helping another woman with the app, but when she was free, Mindy turned to her with a smile. "Did you get it? I know you already know your ancestry, but did you learn anything new?"

"I'm not sure. I think maybe something's wrong."

"Oh? Let me see."

Emma held up her screen. "There's no Italian on here at all."

"Hmm..." Mindy took the phone from her. "Could Italian be included in this Northwestern European section?"

Emma shook her head. "Even if it was, that's only about twenty percent of the whole pie. My dad was probably one hundred percent Italian—and his parents before him. So shouldn't I be at least fifty percent?"

Mindy studied the graphs on Emma's phone. "That is strange."

"Could mine have gotten mixed up with somebody else's?" Other women had found DNA matches—cousins or second cousins once removed— of relatives who'd also had their DNA tested. Emma hadn't expected to find those kind of connections since both of her parents and she, too, were only children. But she'd never expected *this*.

"I'll check with my brother," Mindy said. "But I wouldn't think there's a mix-up. These tests are usually very accurate. But I suppose anything's possible. I'll have Gavin check into it. Oh, hang on…" Her eyes lit and she dug in the book bag she always carried to their meetings. "I had one test left over. I think it's still in here…" A few seconds later she produced a packet identical to the one they'd all used. "Just take that home and repeat the same steps we did, then send it directly to the address they provide."

"Are you sure no one else needs it?"

"No, it's an extra. Gavin probably won't be the one who handles it this time, so it might take longer to get the results back, but you won't have to pay for it again or anything."

"Thanks, Mindy. I appreciate that. Tell Gavin thanks." She tucked the test in her purse, not even sure she would bother to use it. But probably. It already bugged her that the test had been so far off. It had to be a mix-up in the lab. Which didn't give her much confidence in Gavin's company. How many other people had gotten faulty results and just assumed they were correct? If you didn't already know your ancestry, a mistake like this could be devastating. Life-changing even. But of course, she couldn't say any of that to Mindy. Instead, she thanked her again and went to find Julia.

"So, did you send it in?" Tadhg rested his wrist on the steering wheel and cocked his head, waiting for her answer.

It was one of the things Emma loved most about him. He seemed genuinely interested in her life. When she'd told him about the mix-up with the ancestry test results on the way to church this morning, he was almost angry on her behalf.

"I put it in my mailbox the morning after book club, so it's only been a week. Maybe it's dumb to redo it, but it really bugged me that it was wrong."

"It would have bugged me too."

"Even though you know your ancestry?"

"*Especially* because I know it." He affected a Dublin Irish brogue. "Shore 'tisn't the sort of information a body be messin' with."

She laughed, adoring the brogue and this playful side of him. And feeling better about her decision to redo the test.

The light turned green and he crossed the intersection headed in the direction of her house. "You're sure you don't want to grab some fast food? I hate making you cook on Sunday."

"Not if you're okay with leftover lasagna. Mom always leaves me with enough for a small army. And my freezer is already over-flowing."

He gave a sharp salute in her direction. "Yes, ma'am. You'll get no argument from me."

"And I have New York style cheesecake for dessert."

"Definitely no argument. And don't forget you promised me a tour of the farm."

She laughed. "That'll take about two seconds. Unless we stop to pull weeds."

His expression turned serious. "Oh, I don't believe in working on Sundays."

She tossed a half smile his way. "Nice save."

"Besides I wouldn't want to get my church clothes dirty." He looked down at his khaki shorts and T-shirt, which passed for church attire at most services on the island—certainly at the little community church she'd attended all her life.

She smiled but didn't comment the rest of the way home. In truth, she was a little nervous about having him over to her house. She'd cleaned for two solid hours after book club last night while she waited for the cheesecake to bake. The gardens were already at their best this time of year before the weeds had a chance to take over. Still, inviting him to her house implied some kind of... *commitment* that she wasn't sure she was quite ready for.

But here they were. He turned into the driveway and she pointed to where he should park, behind her Malibu.

They climbed out and he walked slowly toward the front porch, taking in the house and yard. She followed him, trying to see things with his eyes. The front porch could use a fresh coat of paint, but the Carolina Jessamine hid that fact well this time of year. There were only a few of the yellow blooms remaining, but the slender leaves made an attractive vine.

"Nice place," he said at the door. "You're really lucky."

"I'm really *blessed*," she corrected. "When I was a kid, I always dreamed about living in this house someday. And here I am." She didn't tell him that she wanted to raise her own children in this house.

He nodded and followed her inside. He stopped at the view of the backyard through the bank of windows. His reaction was the same as Julia's had been when she first saw it—and it wasn't even sunset yet. "This is like some kind of hidden treasure. Do people know this is here?"

"Well, some people, obviously. I mean, it's not a secret or anything."

Bud trotted in from the kitchen, tail held high.

Tadhg immediately stooped to pet the cat. "This must be the famous Rosebud."

"Shhh..." She put a finger to her lips. "He gets a little insulted when you call him that. He prefers to go by just Bud."

He played along. "Sorry, buddy...er, I mean just Bud, you manly cat, you."

She laughed as Tadhg kicked off his shoes and set them by the front door, then scooped Bud into his arms and went to look out the windows.

"You grew all those flowers yourself?" He motioned to the yard beyond.

"Oh, this is nothing. Wait till you see it a month from now. There's hardly anything in bloom right now. But to answer your question, I planted a lot of them, but my grandparents planted the tulips and azaleas and most of the other perennials. I'm just the caretaker of those. But the raised beds are all mine."

"Looks like you're doing a good job."

"Well, it *is* my job, so I'd better."

"But you love what you do?"

"I really do. I mean, there are certain times of year when it's not so fun. I'm not a fan of the heat and humidity in July and August. But it's mostly very rewarding."

"I think it's cool."

She smiled. "Thanks. I do too. Now let's get that lasagna heated up."

"What can I do to help?"

She led the way to the kitchen and handed him two glasses. "You can fill these with ice and pour some Coke—or whatever you want to drink. I have fizzy water, or I think there's a bottle of wine in the fridge that someone gave me as a thank-you for doing their wedding flowers. We can open that if you'd like."

He held up a hand and winced. "Thanks, but...apparently, I don't handle alcohol all that well. Coke will be great."

"Oh. Of course. Sorry, I should have—"

"No, it's okay. Some people can handle it. Maybe I could now, but I'd rather not take any chances."

He said it all so matter-of-factly that it put her instantly at ease. She cut two generous slices of lasagna, covered them, and put them in the microwave to heat, then sliced and buttered some store-bought French bread, wrapped it in foil, and slid it in the oven. "Let's eat out on the loggia. There's a fruit salad in the fridge. You can carry that and our drinks out. I'll bring our plates when it's ready."

"Sure. Hate to waste such a beautiful day indoors."

When she came out with plates of lasagna and bread a few minutes later, Tadhg had claimed the chair in the corner. He had his bare feet propped on the railing and was sipping his Coke, Bud curled up underneath his chair.

"That smells good." He quickly put his feet under the table and pivoted to face her. "Thanks."

When she was seated, he asked, "Can I pray for the meal?"

"Of course." She bowed her head.

"Father God, thank you for this beautiful Sunday and for the beautiful girl sitting across from me." He paused and when she peeked, he was looking back at her, obviously waiting for a reaction.

She blushed and smiled her thanks.

"And thank you for this good food. Amen."

"You might want to taste it before you declare it good."

"I'm not worried." Grinning, he took a napkin from the short stack she'd carried out and folded it in his lap. The way he made himself at home here made him easy to be with. And she couldn't help the thought that came: She wouldn't mind having this man on her porch, in her house, on a regular basis.

Maybe on a permanent basis.

Chapter Seven

"So, what are these pink ones?" Tadhg bent to smell the fluffy blooms on a bush near the woods behind Emma's house. Except for buying a bouquet in a flower shop or at the farmers market for some girl, he'd never really cared about flowers or plants. But Emma's enthusiasm somehow caused him to be genuinely intrigued.

"Those are azaleas. That's like what you bought from me at the farmers market. Remember? The ones you gave to your 'girlfriend.' They're just about done blooming though."

He moved slowly to a raised bed near the bushes and tried to change the subject by asking about the flowers growing there. "These are some kind of tulip, right?" They looked similar to the ones she'd given him for Izzy, but these had fancy edges.

"Yes. Tulips. That's what you gave your so-called grandma. Except these are a fringed variety."

He ducked his head. "You're never going to let me live that down, are you?"

He meant it as a joke, but she didn't laugh or even smile.

"They're pretty," he said after her silence became uncomfortable.

"They are. I like them because they bloom a little later in the spring than regular tulips. At least this variety." Her chilly demeanor warmed a little. "I wish tulips lasted longer. But I think they sell so well partly because they're so fleeting. And they're one of the first things to bloom in the spring. If it wasn't for the azaleas and tulips, I wouldn't have much to offer at the market until later in the season."

He straightened and surveyed the backyard. "It's pretty amazing what you've done here. Seriously."

She looked pleased with the compliment. "It's a lot of work, but it's worth it. I just wish my grandparents could see all this now."

"They would be very proud of you."

The last of the frost thawed and she beamed. "Thanks. And I hope you get to see it about a month from now when things are really blooming."

"Yeah, me too." He wiped sweat from his brow with the back of his hand.

"That sun is hot. Let's go sit in the shade."

He followed her back to the porch, grateful for the sea breeze wafting through.

"You ready for some cheesecake yet?"

"I was afraid you'd forgotten," he admitted.

She rolled her eyes comically. "I did not slave over a hot stove for two hours only to forget to serve that bad boy."

He laughed, relieved, his mouth watering.

"Do you want coffee or something cold to drink with it?"

"Coffee would be awesome. Need help?"

"Sure. You can slice the cheesecake while I make coffee."

Inside, she took the golden-brown dessert from the fridge and handed him a knife. "Don't be stingy. And I'll send some home with you too."

They worked in comfortable silence, and a few minutes later, carried heavy plates and steaming mugs back to what she called the loggia, where they'd eaten lunch.

He swallowed a bit of the creamy, sweet-but-not-too-sweet

confection. "This is delicious. Like something you'd order in a restaurant."

"It's my specialty. And it's really not that hard to make. It just takes a long time to bake."

"So, you didn't *really* slave over a hot stove?"

"Well, not for two hours anyway. That was hyperbole." She grinned.

He was tempted to point out that calling Izzy his grandma had also been hyperbole, but he decided not to risk bringing up the topic and having her turn frosty again. Instead, he grinned back at her and settled into his chair, enjoying the perfect Sunday afternoon.

They talked for two hours watching the sky as banks of cumulous clouds floated lazily by, the sun peaking out from time to time just enough to toast the breezes. She was saying something about her college days at Georgia Southern in Savannah.

"Wait..." He sat up straighter. "I thought you didn't go to college."

"I didn't graduate. I went two semesters. Lived at home. But even with just tuition, it seemed stupid to pay for a degree when I already knew what I wanted to do."

"Which was this?" He swept an arm to encompass the backyard.

"Yes." She frowned. "I kind of wish I could get back the money I paid for tuition and books. I could have bought a lot of soil and fertilizer for what I paid."

"Tell me about it. And I went five semesters. And lived on campus."

"Ouch. Do you still have student loans?" She held up a hand. "If that's not too personal."

It was, but he'd incriminate himself if he said so. He was embarrassed that he still had debt for a degree that had never materialized. "I have a couple, but they're almost paid off." *Almost* was a relative term, but with all the overtime he was working, he might get them both paid off by Christmas. He'd done pretty well with his consignment stuff this month, and thanks to that side hustle, his savings account was growing. But he was determined not to touch that for anything but its intended purpose. He just prayed his stupid truck was still running by Christmas.

"Do you think you'll ever go back and get that teaching degree?" The way her hazel eyes widened with anticipation, he could tell she hoped he would.

He shook his head. "I doubt it. I don't think any of my classes would transfer. And honestly, I'm not sure I have what it takes to teach."

"Your major in college was business, right?"

"Which year?"

She tilted her head, questioning.

"It started out as Business just because I didn't know *what* I wanted to do. By the time I switched to Education, I was four semesters in and pretty disillusioned with school. Probably because my grades were pathetic. And that was back when I was working hard to mess up my life. So when I got offered the job here, it was an easy out." That was the truth and nothing but the truth.

But it wasn't the whole truth.

"I should probably go." Tadhg started to rise, then sat back down laughing. "That's about the fifth time I've said that, isn't it?"

"Sixth." She grinned, loving that he didn't seem to want to leave. "But who's counting?"

"I really should go though."

"Don't go on my account. You're not keeping me from anything."

She wanted him to stay in the worst way. They'd talked about everything from his job to her farm to the families they grew up in to the books they were reading. She was delighted to learn that he was a reader too, even though his taste ran more toward history and technology while she preferred a good novel. "Might as well learn something while I'm reading," he'd quipped.

"What? You don't think you can learn anything reading a novel?"

"Not anything true."

"I disagree. I've found more truth in some novels than a lot of the so-called self-help books I've read." She hesitated. "Not that I've read a lot of self-help books, but you know what I mean."

"No. I don't. Novels are fiction. Fiction means 'not true.' What am I missing?"

That had led to a half hour discussion that got heated in the best possible way.

In the gathering twilight, they moved to the porch swing and talked until the sun slipped below the treetops. She liked Tadhg McKay more and more with every topic they covered.

It was after eleven—and second slices of cheesecake—when he finally said, "I might not be keeping you from anything, but some of us have to work tomorrow." He held up a hand. "I know, I know... You probably have to work too, although it must be nice to be your own boss. Get to make your own hours."

"Well, kind of. But if I don't get outside early, the heat is a beast. And I can't really take off two days in a row or the weeds take over. And even though I can design bouquets in my kitchen after dark, if I don't get the flowers cut before dark, I have nothing to sell at the market. And all bets are off if it's a wedding weekend and I have to do flowers, so—" She caught the wry grin he gave her. "I'll shut up now. I didn't mean to get defensive."

He looked sheepish. "No, I had that coming. I truly wasn't implying that you don't work hard. I just—"

"I know you weren't." She gave an apologetic smile.

"I'm just jealous that you love what you do so much."

"You don't?"

He shrugged. "It's a job. It pays the bills."

"Then why don't you find something you love? My dad

always said if you work at what you love, you'll never work a day in your life."

"Mark Twain said that. Or something like it."

"Really?" She giggled. "I thought that was original to my dad." Her father probably wasn't aware the quote came from Twain. He'd never been much for reading. Not like Mom.

"You must have been a daddy's girl."

She thought for a minute. "I suppose I was. Maybe all only children are. But back on the subject—seriously, Tadhg, if you want to be a teacher, go back to school."

He shook his head and became preoccupied with an oak leaf that had landed on the floor of the loggia. He leaned over and picked it up, twirling it back and forth between his fingers. "No," he finally said, still studying the leaf. "I think that ship has sailed."

"No way. Lots of people change careers when they're way older than you are." She didn't tell him that she'd never understood why someone would stay at a job they didn't enjoy.

He shrugged again, not meeting her eyes. He fished his phone from his pocket and checked the time. "I really should go."

"Oh." His abruptness took her by surprise.

He slowly stopped the swing's sway and rose awkwardly. "Thanks for the great lunch."

His smile appeared genuine, so why did it seem like he was breaking up with her before there was even anything to break? Feeling a strange sense of desperation, she said, "Hey, do you want to take home the last piece of lasagna? It'll just get thrown out otherwise."

"No, that's okay. Let Bud have it."

The cat had slept at Tadhg's feet on the loggia most of the day, but now Bud rose and stretched, arching his back like a Halloween cut-out.

"Thanks, but he's not much for table scraps. Oh, but don't you want to take some cheesecake home?"

"I'm good. Thanks."

"Bud won't eat cheesecake either."

Tadhg acted as if he hadn't heard her and started toward the door. She followed him inside and through the house to the front door in silence, watching as he stepped into his shoes, his focus on the sandals as if they were some new contraption he'd never seen before. Finally, he straightened and twisted the doorknob. "Well... thanks again," he said over one shoulder.

"Sure." She didn't want to use the word *goodbye*. But she couldn't say "see you later" either because she wasn't sure she would.

What had happened to change the warmth of five minutes ago? Had she said something that offended him? If she'd had any claim on him, she would have stopped him. Not let him leave without telling her what was wrong. But that was just it—she *didn't* have any claim on him. None whatsoever.

So she stood on the front porch in silence and watched him climb into his pickup. She dared to hope he would turn and wave as he backed out of the driveway. Or even that he'd jump out of the truck and explain what she'd said that had caused him to close up tighter than a morning glory at night.

But he did neither. He backed out of the driveway, his face lost in the evening shadows, and the taillights of his pickup faded into the night.

She went back inside feeling as if she'd lost her best friend. She was being ridiculous. She barely knew this guy. But stupidly, she'd thought he might turn out to be someone special. Maybe even *the* someone.

"God, don't let me be foolish," she whispered. "I only want the one you want for me."

Bud moseyed over and meowed up at her, as if he thought she'd been talking to him. That made her laugh. But picking up the purring cat, loneliness overwhelmed her and she let the tears fall. They weren't tears of grief or even sadness—just deep disappointment that something she'd thought was coming into full bloom had instead wilted and shriveled.

Chapter Eight

Tadhg parked the company vehicle in the lot and headed toward the office. It had been a frustrating Monday morning with grumpy customers and equipment that didn't work. He headed back to the office he shared with two other technicians, hoping he'd have the space to himself for a few minutes.

No such luck. Jason was parked at his desk looking over the dispatch log. "Hey, bro, you back already?"

"I'm not done. I left my stupid multimeter at the last house and by the time I realized it, they were already gone for the day. Came back to grab another one, but I'm going to get some lunch first."

Not waiting for a reply from his coworker, he went to check his assignments. "What's up with this?" Jillian had piled a day and a half worth of appointments on him and Jason.

Jason rolled his eyes. "Apparently Brian went home sick after his first call."

"For real? That's the second time this month." He slammed his desk drawer closed harder than necessary.

"Tell me about it. At least you don't have a wife to give you grief when you don't get home till seven o'clock every night. Bree has about had it with all this overtime."

"Did you talk to Jillian?"

"Not yet. She'll just tell us to get over it. It comes with the job description."

That was true. Their office manager took the attitude that anybody on her docket ought to just be grateful they had a job at all. Tadhg wouldn't tell Jason, but he was grateful for the overtime. The extra money would help him put a considerable dent in his student loans. And the extra work hours meant less time to sit at home and moan about Emma.

He'd blown it last night. Shut down as soon as she brought up the subject of him going back to get his teaching degree. He should have just told her the truth. He *should* have. But he liked this girl. Liked her a lot. He'd already been forced to tell her about his sordid past long before he wanted to.

In truth, it was a relief to have that story out of the way. That was the big one. The one that had ended more than one relationship. But Emma hadn't freaked out or told him to take a hike or even seemed upset. Unlike some of the women he'd dated, she'd believed him when he assured her that was all in the past.

But sometimes, as bad as you wanted past things to stay in the past, they followed you and haunted you. He had no one to blame but himself and it wasn't something he couldn't navigate. But explaining all the gory details to Emma might prove to be too much. Might push her over the edge. Besides, it wasn't the kind of thing you sprang on a woman you'd only known for three weeks.

And niggling at the back of his consciousness was a little detail he'd become practiced at concealing. His mouth had been trained to say that line... *I never killed anybody or went to prison...* Like too many lines he spouted whenever he told his story, it was strategically constructed to be true. One hundred percent true. But he wasn't so naive about his own guile that he didn't know his words were carefully composed to conceal another truth that didn't exonerate him quite so conveniently.

But he at least owed Emma an explanation of why he'd been so short with her last night. He pulled up the company app and glanced over his log again. Shoot! Jillian had added another stop to his list since he sat down five minutes ago. He'd be lucky if he got home before eight tonight.

But he would call Emma. Tomorrow night. Just keep it casual, but at least he'd let her know he was still interested. Because he was pretty sure by her demeanor when he left last night that she thought she'd never hear from him again.

He knew that feeling all too well and he didn't want to do the same to sweet Emma Fiori. Just the thought of her made him smile.

"What's so funny, man?" Jason eyed him with curiosity.

"Funny? Oh...nothing. Just..." He held up his phone. "Something on my phone."

"Whatever." Jason scraped back his chair and grabbed his gear. "My last appointment's out by my place, so I'm not coming back to the office tonight. See you tomorrow."

Tadhg gave a half wave. "See you tomorrow."

A pang of conscience twisted his gut. He didn't owe Jason any information about his dating life, but he didn't have to lie to the guy about what had made him smile. Sure, it was a little thing. A white lie. No harm done, but it was what his dad would have called a "flat-out lie"—one that, no matter his intention, was simply not the truth.

Ever since Emma had called him on telling her he was giving those flowers to his "grandma," he'd been convicted about his penchant for stretching the truth. What he'd said to cover for his lie—that Izzy was like a grandmother to him—was totally true. And it was true he'd said it in the spirit of joking and flirting with her. But he *had* implied something that wasn't true.

And he could tell it had bothered her. And that bothered him. He'd been praying for help to be more honest. For sure no more flat-out lies. Even when he was teasing. And even if he didn't burden her with *all* his secrets quite yet, he would apologize sincerely for the Grandma Izzy lie. He owed her that.

EMMA WASHED her muddy feet off with the garden hose by the back door. She dried her hands and checked her phone, disappointed when there was nothing from Tadhg. But there was nothing like getting her hands in the dirt to make her problems seem smaller. The gardens were looking good and she would have plenty of flowers for Saturday's market.

Still, she hoped Tadhg would call again. Hoped she'd been mistaken about how distant he'd been when he left last night. But she wasn't going to call him. If it was meant to be, it would happen. The ball was in his court now. She wouldn't force things.

She scrolled quickly through her emails, then walked around the house and down the drive to the mailbox. The afternoons had started to warm up and she lifted sweat-damp hair off her neck, relishing the cool sea breeze on her skin. The mailbox held an Amazon packet—probably the pumpkin seeds she'd ordered— and the usual stack of garden catalogs and restaurant coupons. But one envelope caught her eye.

Surely her do-over DNA test results weren't back already. Besides, those were supposed to come via email first. She tore the envelope open.

The same sheet they'd gotten with their tests at the library that night was inside, but there was also a hand-written note. Odd. She unfolded it and read.

Hello, Emma,

My sister, Mindy Bryson, mentioned that you thought maybe your test results were in error so I personally handled your second test. The results came up identical to what your first test showed so I feel certain the results are accurate. If you have any other questions, feel free to reach out and I'll help if I can. I hope your book club group enjoyed the activity.

Sincerely,
Gavin Ellison

She looked at the accompanying sheet and pulled up the results on her phone with the new code. He was right. The graphs were identical to the ones she'd received the first time. This couldn't be right.

On a whim, she dialed her mom, who answered on the first ring.

"Hey sweetie, what's up?"

"Hey, Mom. I just had something weird happen and—"

"Weird? In what way?"

"Well, you know those DNA tests we took for book club?"

Silence on her mother's end. Finally she said, "Yes..." Then under her breath, "I hate those things."

"What? Why?"

"Oh, I just don't trust them. They just seem like another way to get your money. There's no way to know if they're really accurate, and I've heard too many stories where they just caused trouble."

"Trouble? What do you mean?"

"Well, you're the one who told me somebody got killed because of one of those tests."

She laughed. "Mom, that was a novel. It didn't really happen."

"Well, it could." Mom cleared her throat. "How's the garden doing?"

"It's looking good. I just finished weeding, but you know how that goes. It'll need it again in two days."

"I still say you ought to sell the place."

"No... I love this place. But wait. Back to why I called. I've done my test two different times now and both times it came up the same, except there's no Italian in my background. I mean like zero. How could that be? Dad wasn't adopted or something, was he?" She was halfway kidding, but once the words were out, it struck her that it *could* be true. She knew that back in her parents' day adoptions were sometimes kept secret.

"Dad? No, of course not. Why would you think that?"

"I told you. There is no Italian in my DNA. That means if Dad wasn't adopted, he couldn't be my father."

"Well, we both know your dad was as Italian as they come."

"I know. That's why it's so weird."

"I'm telling you, honey, those things are a waste of money. Just forget about it. I can't believe you paid for that twice."

"I didn't. There was an extra one and Mindy let me take it home."

"Oh, well, that's good. So, what's your little game for the next book club? I don't think you mentioned it."

"Mom?" Something was wrong. Her mother kept changing the subject, and she was acting stranger than strange. "Is there something you're not telling me?"

"What do you mean?"

"Mom, I'm serious. What is going on?"

"I just don't like you getting all worked up about a silly test. Those things are hit-or-miss." Mom was *definitely* dodging her questions.

"No. They're not, Mom. They're actually quite accurate. And that's not what I'm worked up about."

"What then?"

"Because I think there's something you're not telling me. Is —" She couldn't bring herself to even speak the words, but it seemed to be a fact that there was no Italian in her DNA. If Dad wasn't actually her father then who was? "Is Dad my father? My birth father?"

"Emma, I don't want to talk about this on the phone. It's not—"

"On the *phone*? Then there *is* something to talk about. Is that what you're saying? Dad isn't my father?" Her voice lifted an octave and she couldn't help the groan that rose in her throat.

"Your dad was the best father possible, Emma. You know that. And don't you ever believe otherwise."

She was afraid she was going to faint. "Mom...are you saying Dad wasn't my biological father? Answer me!" *This couldn't be happening.*

"Emma, don't speak to me in that tone. We'll talk about this. I promise. But not over the phone."

"Oh, dear God!" It came out as a wail. "You're serious then. Daddy isn't my real father."

"Emma, stop it! Of course he was. He would be devastated to hear the way you're talking."

Her fingernails dug into the flesh of her palms. "You're avoiding answering my question. That's not fair, Mom, and you know it." She'd never been so disrespectful, but how could Mom not understand how important this was to her?

"Emma, calm down. Let's have lunch soon and we'll talk."

"I'm driving up right now."

"No. You'll get stuck in rush hour. Just wait..." Her mother sighed deeply. "Oh, all right. I'll make us a nice dinner. I have some leftover brisket I can heat up. Bill has a meeting at the church tonight so he won't be here."

Emma was relieved to hear that. She liked Mom's husband, but this was a conversation for just the two of them. "I need to take a quick shower. I'm a sweaty mess. But I'll be there before six."

SHE HUNG UP THE PHONE, trembling. The day she'd dreaded for almost three decades now, the day she'd hoped would never *come had come after all. Why hadn't she done something—anything—to keep Emma from taking that stupid test.*

"Caroline? Everything okay, babe?" Bill stood in the doorway, his face a mask of concern.

"I'm fine. Emma's coming over. She knows."

"Knows? Everything?"

"No. Of course not. She can never know...everything. But she re-took the test and she knows that...she was adopted. There was no Italian in her DNA. Zero."

"So, what are you going to tell her?"

She rubbed her forehead as if it might stop her mind from racing. "I'll tell her as much as I can."

"Do you want me to be here?" He sat down beside her on the sofa and put an arm around her shoulder.

"No, you can't miss your meeting." She slumped against him, finding comfort in his strength as she always had. She was so blessed to have him. She'd never thought she would remarry after Tony. William Chambers had been a surprise, a gift.

"You're sure?"

She nodded. "I wish I'd just lied. Emma gave me the perfect out."

"What do you mean?"

"She asked if Tony was adopted. I wish I'd just said yes. That would have been such a simple answer. One that wouldn't have changed anything."

"No, Caroline. You don't want to go down that road. You know what a tangled web one lie can become."

She sighed. "I know. But...it would have satisfied Emma. And it wouldn't be nearly as traumatic as...as the truth. Even what little I can tell her of it."

And until now, she had told the truth. Not always the whole truth, but she had answered Emma's questions—surprisingly few questions over the years—in a way that was truthful, at least on the surface. Bill was the only other living soul who knew the whole story. And she trusted him with every molecule of her being.

He squeezed her shoulder. "It might take some time, but Emma's a strong girl. She'll be okay."

Would she though? It must feel like an awful betrayal. And she *would be able to answer so few of the questions Emma was bound to have—and still keep the promises she'd made all those years ago. Could her daughter forgive what she would never know?*

Chapter Nine

Traffic was a bear on I-95, just as Mom predicted, but Emma knew she wouldn't sleep a wink until she'd talked to her and found out... *What?* What awful truth about herself was she about to discover?

She shuddered and pushed the cruise control up a notch as she passed Savannah's city limits sign.

She parked in the driveway of Mom and Bill's home in the Georgetown neighborhood and rang the doorbell.

When her mother answered the door, it was clear she'd been crying.

Her pulse raced. "Mom?"

"Oh, honey." Mom took her into her arms and a taut thread of fear wound itself around Emma's heart.

She pulled away. "What is it? Please tell me."

"Come in and have some supper first."

"I really don't have an appetite. Not until I know what is going on."

"Well at least let me get you something to drink. I can keep the brisket warm for a while."

Emma didn't argue and went out to the patio where they

always sat if the weather was nice enough. She curled up on the wicker settee, feeling faint.

She heard ice clattering into glasses and then the pop top of a can opening and that familiar hiss. San Pellegrino. Her mom knew her better than anyone in the world. Knew that barbecued brisket was her favorite meal, that she drank cheap sparkling water at home, but preferred San Pellegrino. It hurt to have some secret hanging between them. One she felt sure would change her life.

Mom appeared with two glasses and handed her one with a cocktail napkin before sitting in her usual spot in the chair that matched the settee.

"So, how is everything?"

Emma stared at her. "Seriously? Mom. Stop. Just tell me."

Her mother took a sip of her drink and closed her eyes. "First of all, you need to know that you were *our* baby from the minute you were placed in my arms. Nothing will ever change that. Your dad and I have been your parents—your true parents since you took your first breath in the hospital."

"Wait. *Your dad and I?* So you're saying I'm...adopted." Her voice wavered.

The silence lengthened and her imagination with it. For some reason, she'd assumed it was only her dad's paternity in question. She'd started to suspect that he'd been adopted. After all, Mom's Scottish and English heritage had shown up, as expected, in the test. With all the possibilities that had swirled through her brain in the hours since she'd gotten that stupid test back, she'd even wondered if her mom had an affair, or God forbid, had been raped. But now it seemed clear. *Neither* of her "parents" were her birth parents.

She said as much once she found her voice. "So I'm...adopted. But you said *before* I took my first breath. So, you were there when I was born?"

"Yes." She didn't elaborate.

Emma's cheeks grew warm. "*Yes?* That's it? That's all I get after—" She took a calming breath. "Mom, were you there in the delivery room?"

Mom hesitated a second too long. "Yes."

But Emma read something in her eyes, something she wasn't saying. "So if you were in the delivery room, that means you know my birth mother. I want to meet her." She wasn't at all sure she really did. And she was chagrined to realize that she'd only said it to hurt her mom. The way this long-hidden secret was hurting her.

"That isn't possible, honey."

"What do you mean it isn't possible?" But Mom's words confirmed it. The woman sitting here, the woman she'd thought was her mother for her entire life, suddenly felt like a stranger. And shared not a drop of blood with her. "Why isn't it possible?"

"She..." Mom teared up and her voice broke. "Your...birth mother passed away."

Emma gasped. "What? When?"

"A few years ago."

"Why would you do this? How could you keep this from me?" Her hands trembled in a way that scared her. "You took away any chance I had to know her."

"I didn't know she was going to die. And you were still... young when it happened."

"I don't care. I should have been able to decide for myself. You robbed me of knowing my mother!"

Her mother flinched as if she'd been struck. But she didn't care. Her head throbbed and a horrific thought came. "How did she die? Was it something hereditary? Cancer? Is it something I need to be tested for?"

"No, honey. No, nothing like that." Mom reached to pat her knee.

But Emma curled up tighter in the corner of the chair, denying her. "I need to know my medical history. You at least owe me that."

"We did think about that, Emma, and I can tell you anything

you need to know about your medical history. If you ever need to know."

"Of course, I need to know. I need to know *now*! How can you think I wouldn't want that information? *Need* it? When did she die?"

"If there was anything that would make a difference, I would have told you. I would never do anything to put you in danger or to hurt you. Surely you know that."

She spoke in a monotone. "And you don't think *this* hurts me?"

Her mother just dropped her head and stared at her lap.

Emma forced herself to calm down. "So you know my history?"

"I know some of it. Your birth parents—" She stopped mid-sentence, and for a minute Emma thought she was going to cry. But then she swallowed hard and continued. "I can tell you that there is nothing serious in your history. Your medical history. No cancer, no diabetes, no dementia that I'm aware of...truly nothing serious at all."

"But she's dead? She couldn't have been that old. So how could you even know her history?" Her mind raced. "What was her name? And what about my father? My biological father?"

Mom started shaking her head. "I'm not going to go into any details, Emma. The important thing is that she gave you a chance at life. And you have a good life, honey. Had a good childhood. A father—and a mother—who loved you more than life itself. Who would have done anything for you. And if not for us, you would be an orphan now."

An orphan? "So, my *father* is dead too? My birth father? When? When did they die?" She bit her tongue hard to keep from saying something she'd regret. To keep from telling her mother that she *was* an orphan now as far as she was concerned. "But...I have my birth certificate. It's your name and Dad's on there."

"Exactly. Because we *are* your parents. We always have been. From the moment you were born. You couldn't have been more our own if I'd given birth to you myself. Your adoption was complete even before you were born, and we did everything in our power to give you a good life, a happy childhood. We would have given our very lives for you! And I still would. You know that, Emma."

"I just don't understand why you didn't tell me. I'm twenty-seven years old and you've kept this from me my whole life? We're not living in the dark ages, you know. It's not like adoption is some shameful secret." But that's exactly what it felt like right now.

"Emma, all I can say is that we had our reasons. And I stand by them."

"You know what I mean, Mom."

"And I hope you know what *I* mean." Mom rose and went inside, leaving their glasses on the patio table.

Stunned by the outright rejection, Emma grabbed the glasses and followed her inside. The aroma of Mom's famous brisket wafted under her nose but instead of making her mouth water, the smell turned her stomach.

Without acknowledging her, her mother grabbed a dishcloth out of the sink. She waited for the water to get hot, then rinsed the rag and squeezed out the water. Steam rose from the sink, but Mom just stood there, rinsing the rag over and over.

"Are you just going to ignore me?" Unexpectedly, Emma's voice fractured. She couldn't ever remember a time that she and her mom were so at odds. It hurt.

"I'm not ignoring you." She squeezed the rag out one last time and turned off the water. "I just don't have anything else to say."

"How can you say that? I've been lied to my whole life and now you're just going to leave it at that?" Her voice came out in an odd squeak.

Mom turned to her, her usually pretty face haggard and drawn. "Emma, we never lied to you. No, we may not have told you the whole truth, but we never lied. Your dad and I were firm about that. We never wanted you to accuse us if—" She clipped off the sentence as if she hadn't meant to say so much.

"If what? If I found out the truth? Is that what you were going to say?"

For the first time all evening, Mom met her gaze. "We never intended you to find out. We only wanted to be truthful with as much as we *could* say. Now please stop asking questions. Believe me when I tell you that you know everything you need to know. Most importantly that your dad and I loved you from the second we laid eyes on you. Even before that. Before you were born."

Emma shook her head, bewildered. "You're talking in riddles, Mom. What do you mean you *couldn't* say anything? Why not? This isn't making any sense at all."

"We promised your...birth mother. She made us promise that we would never tell you. And...your dad and I wanted you so very much that we agreed to that promise."

"But— You said she's dead now. Surely she didn't mean for you to go to your grave with a secret like this!"

Mom gave a humorless laugh. "She actually used those very words. She made us promise to go to our graves with it."

"Well, the secret is about *me*, and I can tell you it's wrong. It's ridiculous. I can't live with this, Mom. I can't!"

"Don't be ridiculous." She threw Emma's word back at her. "Of course you can. Nothing—absolutely nothing has changed."

For the briefest moment, Emma thought she saw acknowledgement of the lie of that ludicrous statement in her mother's eyes.

But mom continued, gathering steam. "You are my precious daughter, you grew up in a house full of love. You've made me and your dad more proud than you can know. And you have a whole wonderful life ahead of you. You are blessed to be doing exactly what you want to do—with the gardens, I mean—and someday you'll meet someone wonderful and have babies of your own and—"

"Will I?" The thought came as if she'd been struck by it.

"What if I can't have babies? Is that why you adopted? You couldn't get pregnant? What if I have the same condition...whatever that was." She thought for a minute. "But wait...I thought you and Dad had me right away. No. You *did*." Her mind swam with confusion. Nothing made sense anymore.

The truth was, she'd sometimes suspected that Mom had been pregnant with her when she and Dad got married. They'd eloped and taken a honeymoon to Italy with Nonno and Nonni to visit Dad's extended family. Their wedding anniversary was October 23, and Emma had been born almost exactly eight months later. They'd told her she was born premature. But something didn't add up. "You barely had time to *try* getting pregnant, so why were you looking to adopt?"

Mom fiddled with her wedding ring—the expensive one from Bill—and bowed her head. "Your... Your birth mother was...in trouble and it was a way we could help her. And oh, Emma, I'm so glad we did because after that, we tried to give you a brother or sister and...it just never happened."

"So, you're telling me that practically the day of your wedding you found out about some girl who got pregnant and you offered to adopt her baby? That doesn't even make sense. Who does that?"

Mom laughed, sounding more like herself now. "Well, apparently your dad and I do. And it wasn't the *day* of our wedding."

"But didn't you want some time to just be newlyweds and enjoy life?" She felt like she was talking about some complete stranger.

"Not as much as we wanted you, sweet girl." Tears came to Mom's eyes and it broke Emma's heart. But she couldn't leave until she knew the truth. This was too important to let go.

"I'm...thankful. I really am. But Mom, I'm an adult. I deserve to know the truth about my birth, my history. Put yourself in my place!"

Looking utterly exhausted, Mom sighed. "I know you won't

believe this, but I do understand how you feel. And I'd probably feel the same if I were in your—"

"Then tell me. You *have* to tell me, Mom."

Her mom folded the dish towel in thirds and lopped it over the edge of the sink. She turned with a hardened expression Emma rarely saw on her face. "I *don't* have to. And I'm not going to. I'm sorry. I know you don't like it, but you're just going to have to trust me. The records are sealed, and I have my reasons. And you, Emma, of all people, know that when I make a promise, I keep it. That's all I'm going to say. Now, let's set the table and have some of this brisket I warmed up."

Emma stood there, mouth agape. "You're just going to pretend nothing has changed?"

"Nothing *has* changed, Emma." Mom opened the oven and took out the foil-covered casserole dish. "Do you want some baked beans with yours?"

Stunned and overcome with anger, Emma grabbed her purse from the counter. "No thank you."

Almost dizzy with shock and disbelief, she stormed through the house, let herself out the front door, and still trembling, climbed into her car.

"Emma! Come back here. Right now!"

Though she heard Mom calling her name from the front door, she didn't let herself look back. This sense of betrayal was too great, and the implications of what she'd learned were too much to forgive.

Chapter Ten

Tadhg finished work early for once, but before he went home, he headed to Brunswick to pick up a plant stand he'd found on Facebook Marketplace. The owner was only asking ten dollars and if it was in as good a condition as it appeared to be in the photos, he thought he could refinish it and resell it for five times that. Not that he'd had a ton of extra time on his hands recently, but he'd gone over his finances last night while sleep eluded him, and he'd awakened with a new determination to get his bills paid off and his savings account built up.

He wasn't blind to the fact that one Emma Fiori was the inspiration behind this sudden resolve. He planned to call her as soon as he got home. And he was going for broke. He would ask her out again, and if she said yes and things went well, then he would come clean, tell her everything. If she was the person he thought she was, she'd forgive him and they'd start fresh. Because he liked her. More than he'd liked any woman since Becca.

Half an hour later, with a very cool mid-century plant stand in the back of his truck, he pulled into the driveway. Izzy was in the front yard pulling weeds. He probably should help her—and any other day, he would have—but calling Emma was his priority tonight.

He waved at Izzy and pulled around to his parking spot behind the house. He locked his truck and carried the plant stand up the fire-escape-like stairs to his little apartment. He wasn't into interior design or anything, but he knew what he liked and took pride in the way his apartment had come together. Glancing around the space now—three large rooms plus the small bathroom—he tried to look at it with Emma's eyes.

She would appreciate the books. He'd spent far too much money on books in his lifetime, even though most of them cost only a few dollars each at garage sales or Goodwill. He loved the musty smell they gave his space. It smelled like a library, and he had every intention of continuing to grow his collection.

Emma would also appreciate his much smaller collection of houseplants in front of the kitchen windows, and the stained glass in the transoms over the doors to the bedroom and bath. Plants and stained glass were both compliments of Izzy, but with a little guidance from her, he'd managed to keep the pothos, a schefflera, and two kinds of ficus alive for almost five years now. He hadn't gone so far as to give them names, but he did like the life they gave his little apartment.

His furniture was a mishmash of Facebook Marketplace finds that he'd DIY'd, but everything coordinated nicely and—to his eyes anyway—it looked good. *Homey* was the word Izzy had used the first time she saw what he'd done with the place. Izzy hadn't climbed the steep stairs to his apartment in at least two years. He wasn't sure his elderly landlady could even make the climb anymore.

He wiped the cobwebs off his new antique and set it beside the sofa before foraging in the fridge for supper. He slapped a sandwich together and made a note to get to the grocery store before he starved to death.

When he was finished, he washed the dishes that had collected in the sink, leaving them to dry on the wooden drainer—another Goodwill find. That gave him an idea and before his nerves could stop him, he dialed Emma.

It went straight to voicemail and he hung up without leaving a message.

Disappointed, he went to work on the new plant stand. After lining the floor with layers of newspaper, he gave the piece a light sanding and cleaned it well with mineral spirits. This was always his favorite part of the process when you could see what a piece could become, see the color of the wood and the beauty of the grain.

While he waited for the stand to dry, he dialed Emma again, ready with a voicemail if she didn't pick up. To his surprise, she answered on the first ring.

"Hello?" The hesitation in her voice told him she'd likely put his name in her contacts and knew it was him.

"Hi Emma. It's Tadhg."

"Hi." He couldn't tell if she was pleased to hear from him or not.

"You might not be interested, but I was wondering if you'd want to go shopping with me Friday morning?"

"Shopping? You don't have to work?"

"Oh. Sorry. I should have clarified. Garage sale shopping. They start early. Like seven. But I know you're an early bird. And we could do breakfast afterwards, before I—*we* have to head to work."

"Sounds like fun. But...are we going to fight over the good stuff?"

"I don't know." He smiled to himself. "Maybe. Depends on if we think the same things are good stuff."

"If you liked that pickle jar, I'm afraid we're in trouble."

"I only liked it because I thought you would like it. I didn't know it was a pickle jar though."

"I remember. How about, since you invited me, I'll give you first dibs on anything we would fight over."

He laughed. "It's a deal. I'll pick you up at a quarter till seven?"

"I'll be ready."

"Great." He wasn't ready to hang up, but she didn't seem in a very talkative mood. "You having a good week?"

Silence and then. "To be honest, no."

"Uh-oh. What's going on?"

"It's a long story. I'm still…processing things."

"Do you want to talk about it?"

"Not really… It's complicated. Too complicated for the phone."

"Okay. Well, I'm sorry—for whatever it is." His curiosity ramped up, but he wouldn't push her. "Maybe we can talk about it Friday?"

"Maybe. Thanks. And thank you for calling. I'll see you Friday morning, okay?"

"Sure. See you then."

He waited until the line went dead. Well, that was weird. And a little disappointing. But he had another date with the girl. That was something at least.

EMMA WAS on the porch waiting when Tadhg's pickup rolled up the driveway. She'd almost called and canceled. Since her conversation with Mom, she'd thought of little besides the devastating revelation—and she and her mother hadn't spoken since. But Tadhg was just the distraction she needed. And at least he already knew she'd taken that DNA test, so she wouldn't have to start from square one explaining what had happened. If she even told him.

The last thing she wanted to do was spend the morning crying. And that seemed to be all she could do every time she thought about what she'd learned. The awful revelation that had changed everything. Dad wasn't really her dad. The house she was living in hadn't belonged to her real grandparents. Even her name was a mockery now. She wasn't a Fiori. Not really. And Mom—her adoptive mom—was the only one who could answer her questions, tell her who she really was. And yet she refused. Why?

Tadhg parked the truck in front of the porch, and she pushed the thoughts away. She grabbed her purse off the swing and pasted on a smile.

He leaned across the console and opened the passenger door from inside. "Good morning."

"Good morning. Gosh, it's early." She climbed into the truck and buckled her seatbelt.

When she looked up, he was holding out a paper cup with a colorful sleeve from Wake Up Coffee. She took it from him with a grateful smile. "Bless you."

"I wasn't sure how you drink it, so I just had them put in a little milk and a little sugar." He held his thumb and finger half an inch apart.

"That'll work." She usually drank her coffee black, but she wasn't about to complain. She took a sip and tried to focus on having a fun morning with a guy she really liked. Even though everything felt awkward now. Everything she'd told him about herself—her pride in her Italian heritage, her love of flowers, living in a home that had belonged to people she thought were her grandparents... Maybe if she knew who her real relatives were, she'd feel different, but instead, she felt like a big fake. Like everything she'd ever done in her life had been a sham.

She took a sip of coffee and realized Tadhg had said something. "I'm sorry, what?"

"Not quite awake yet, huh?" His smile said he was teasing. "I thought you were a morning person."

"I don't know what I am." Her eyes watered, and she quickly looked out the side window.

He slowed his truck. "Hey...are you okay?" Concern softened his voice.

She swallowed hard, unable to speak.

He reached across the console and touched her arm briefly. "I don't want to pry, but if you want to talk about it, I'm here."

"Thank you. I...I'm not sure I'm ready to talk. I'm just warning you, I'm probably not going to be very good company."

"It's okay. We don't have to talk. Just drink your coffee and don't mind me."

She gave him an anemic smile, grateful he hadn't pressured her to tell him. And yet, she needed to talk to someone. Mom was the one she usually went to. Or Mindy. But she was afraid her friend might think she was blaming Gavin's company—Mindy's brother—for a faulty test. Though her mother had put to rest any hope she had that the mistake was the lab's.

Tadhg tapped the brakes and Emma looked up to see a garage sale sign at the intersection they were driving through. "You okay with stopping?"

"Of course." She waved off his concern. "That's why we're here."

"I know, but if you're not feeling well..."

She gave him what she hoped was a reassuring smile. "I'm fine. Or I will be. Let's go." She motioned toward the house where half a dozen people were inspecting the goods displayed on the driveway. "Remember, you get first dibs."

"We'll see."

<h1 style="text-align:center">*Chapter Eleven*</h1>

It seemed the harder she tried, the more Emma struggled to be cheerful. She did not want to be a brat and ruin their time together, but she couldn't seem to push her grief aside.

Grief. Until that moment, she hadn't realized that grief was exactly what it was. No one had died, yet it felt like everyone she loved dearest had disappeared from her life. Even Mom, who'd become so distant she might as well live a continent away.

Maybe it was Emma Fiori who'd disappeared. She didn't know who she was any more.

She reached across the console and touched Tadhg's arm the way he'd touched hers earlier. "Can I just tell you what's going on so I can get it off my chest. And then I promise I won't mention it again."

"Emma. Of course. Please. Tell me. Talk about it as much as you want."

"Thank you." The smile she offered felt pasted on. She sighed. "Long story short, I got the results back from that stupid DNA test and it turns out I'm not anything I thought I was." There. She'd said it aloud.

"I don't... I'm not sure I understand."

"I'm adopted. My parents never told me. The reason there

isn't any Italian in my DNA is because I'm *not* Italian. I don't know what I am."

"Oh wow." His eyes grew round. "That's heavy. Why didn't they tell you? Do you know?"

"The only thing my mom said is that she promised my birth mother she wouldn't tell. Ever. Even though she's dead now—my birth mother." She gave him an abbreviated version of her conversation with her mom. "The worst part is that they lied to me. My whole life. I've been thinking back on my childhood...what I thought was a happy childhood. But now I don't know what's true and what was just another lie."

"I'm so sorry, Emma. This must have been such a shock."

"It still is. I've been obsessed with trying to find out the truth. There has to be an original birth certificate out there with the names of my birth parents on it, but Mom said those records are sealed, so I can't get access to them."

"Not to argue, but I guess I can understand why women who put their babies up for adoption might not want to be found."

"But we need our health records and— We just deserve to know! I'm not the only one who thinks that way. When I was searching online, I saw an article from an adoption advocacy group that said some state senator—here in Georgia—is sponsoring a bill that would grant adoptees access to their original birth certificates once they turn eighteen. The original certificate with the birth parents' names. But even if the bill becomes law, it wouldn't go into effect until at least next year. I can't wait that long."

"You may not have a choice, Emma." His voice was gentle and it somehow calmed her.

"I know." She turned to stare out the passenger window.

"But, Emma, none of this changes the fact that you had a happy childhood. And loving parents. Does it? Did...did you ever suspect anything?"

"What do you mean?"

He shrugged. "Growing up. Like, did they ever give you

evasive answers when you asked about your birth? Did you ever wonder why there weren't any pictures of you in the hospital nursery? That kind of thing?"

"No. Maybe I was naive, but I never suspected anything." A memory nudged at the corners of her mind. "Wait a minute... There *are* pictures of me in the hospital! Of Dad holding me. At least Mom said it was the hospital. The pictures are prints, and they're faded, but it looks like a hospital room. But maybe that was a lie too." Had her parents gone so far as to stage photos to bolster their lies? "I don't remember any photos of me with my mom in the hospital, but I *know* she said those pictures with Dad were taken right after I was born."

"Well, if it was an open adoption, your parents might have been at the hospital—with your birth mother—when you were born."

That was true. She couldn't remember if she'd asked Mom about that. Her mind raced, and she desperately wanted to see those pictures again. All her baby photos. Maybe they held some hint of the truth. But would Mom even show them to her now? For all she knew, her mother had combed through them and destroyed them by now, fearing they might hold a hint of the truth. Yet another thing she'd lost.

"Emma? Are you okay?"

She looked over to see a distressed expression on Tadhg's face, and realized she'd been quiet for several minutes. She ran a hand through her hair. "I'm okay. I'm sorry I'm so out of it. I'm not very good company."

"No, it's completely understandable." He paused, then touched her arm again, only this time he left his hand on her wrist, his caress gentle and warm. "Would you rather just go back home?"

"It's probably better if I do something. Get my mind off of it for a while."

"I agree. If you're sure."

She bobbed her head. "I'm sure."

"Then let's find us a good sale."

She felt a little better already. And Tadhg's attitude helped immensely. He didn't seem to think what she'd revealed to him was any big deal.

After striking out at the first sale, he drove past the marina on Newcastle, then slowed at an intersection where three garage sale signs were planted in the ground. "This is more like it."

He coasted past the first one, which she agreed didn't look like it was worth stopping—piles of baby clothes, toys, and paraphernalia. But the next one looked promising with furniture lined up on the driveway and tables overflowing with household items and boxes of books.

He parked behind two other cars in front of the house, and they jumped out and hurried up the driveway. "Remember you promised me first dibs."

She smiled. "I remember."

She felt a little self-conscious having him there as she perused the tables but he soon went inside the garage, leaving her to inspect possibilities without his scrutiny. She chose a couple of candles that had never been lit and a dish towel that still had the tags on it. Inside the garage, once her vision adjusted to the dimmer light, her eye was drawn to a framed watercolor painting leaning against a table. The frame was dusty but in decent shape, and the painting appeared to be an original—a lighthouse with a couple walking on the beach beside it. It wasn't the Saint Simons lighthouse, but a similar one. As she reached for the painting, Tadhg hurried over and took one corner of the frame in his hand.

"Uh-oh." He looked sheepish, but she noticed he made no effort to let go of the painting.

"Are you serious?" She made her tone teasing, but she was disappointed that he was going to fight her for this. It would have looked perfect over the desk in the living room with the natural light that corner of the room received.

"I'm pretty sure I saw it first."

She scoffed and tugged the painting her way. "I'm pretty sure I had my hand on it first."

He yanked it back, grinning. "I'm pretty sure I reminded you of the first dibs rules before we got out of the truck. And you agreed."

She gave a comical harrumph and let go. "I think I see why your name fits so well...Tiger!"

He only shrugged.

She rolled her eyes and moved to another table. After finding a couple other small items, she went to pay for her finds at the table outside.

While she waited at the end of the driveway, Tadhg bargained the seller down five dollars on the painting and paid the woman for it in one dollar bills.

As they walked back to his truck, she shook her head. "All I can say is you'd better have a fabulous place to hang that."

When he didn't reply, she eyed him. "You're not planning to re-sell it are you? Because if you are, I'll pay you what the lady was asking."

He laughed and shook his head. "It's not for sale. I know exactly where it will hang in my apartment. And hey, you knew the rules going in. Besides, who knows, maybe someday we'll share it."

It took her a minute to realize what he meant. And she thought he looked a little embarrassed that he'd said the quiet part out loud. Still, the thought warmed her.

Tadhg opened the passenger door for her, then went around and climbed in behind the steering wheel. But before he started the truck, he turned to her. "I'm really just teasing you. If you want the painting, you can have it. I mean, I like it a lot, but if it's special to you..."

"No, no... You won it fair and square. Like you said, I knew the rules before I got in the vehicle this morning." She wrinkled her nose. "But if you ever get tired of it, don't you dare sell it. I'll buy it from you." Too late, she hoped he didn't think she was refuting his "maybe someday we'll share it" comment.

But he grinned and said, "That's a deal."

At the next place they stopped, she saw him eyeing a baseball glove. She hurried over to grab it before he could. When his face fell, she laughed and handed it to him. "Just kidding. It's yours. I don't have an athletic bone in my body. But if you're going to shop with me, Tiger—and with these rules—you need to work on your poker face."

"Oh, you're cruel. But the joke's on you." He set the glove down where it had been. "This is a lefty glove. I'm not a lefty."

She snapped her fingers. "Shoot!" But her chagrin was feigned. He'd succeeded in lifting her spirits, and she was thankful she'd agreed to come with him.

They stopped at three more sales before he checked the time and frowned. "I hate to ruin a great morning, but I really need to take you home and head for work."

"It's okay. I need to get busy too. The weeds are taking over."

"I can't imagine how you keep up with it."

"Sometimes I don't. I'm doing flowers for a wedding next weekend and that always puts me behind. But stressful as they are, weddings are my bread and butter." She didn't tell him that she was actually glad she'd have the distraction of a wedding.

They drove in silence the rest of the way to her house, and after he parked, he started to get out of the truck—to come around and open her door, she assumed.

She waved him off. "You're sweet to do that, but I don't want to make you late."

He closed his door. "Thanks. It was a fun morning." He motioned with his chin in the direction of the jump seat where he'd tucked the lighthouse painting. "If you're not too mad at me, I'd love to go again next week."

"How about next week *I'll* drive so I get dibs."

He laughed. "I'll give you dibs, but I'd rather take my truck in case I find any furniture."

"Then I'll buy the coffee."

"Deal." He offered his hand across the console and they shook on it.

She gathered the few small things she'd purchased and climbed out of the truck.

But before she could close the door, he leaned across the seat, took her hand, and squeezed it. "I'm really sorry about what happened. The test, I mean. If you need to talk, you have my number." He tapped his phone in his breast pocket.

"Thanks, Tadhg. I appreciate that. I do."

"I'm sure everything will turn out okay. Just talk to your mom again. Don't let this come between you."

Easy for him to say. She nodded and closed the door. She appreciated the sentiment, but he couldn't know that everything would be okay. She didn't see how anything could ever be okay again.

The cool morning air seemed to have evaporated and she felt the suffocating humidity envelop her.

She didn't have time to go to her mom's today, but she was obsessed with the thought of those photos. If Mom hadn't already destroyed them, she needed to see them again. And felt certain they would reveal something that was being hidden from her.

Chapter Twelve

As he went through the motions at work, Tadhg felt the weight of his secret heavier than ever. He had fully intended to come clean with Emma—if not while they were together this morning, then he'd planned to ask her for a date this weekend and tell her then.

But how could he burden her with his miserable secret when she'd been hurt so deeply—and recently—by secrets. By the very sin he was guilty of—*lies and deceit.*

For a long time he'd told himself that his secrets weren't hurting anyone, except maybe himself. But now, even that was a lie. He'd lied to himself so long that he couldn't even admit to himself what he really wanted to do with his life. Because his foolishness had erased so many possibilities.

There was no such thing as a little white lie. Lies were all darkness and evil. And the damage they inflicted usually fell on the ones you loved the most. Lies had distanced him from his parents, from his brothers. Probably, if he were honest, they'd had much to do with why he'd lost Becca. Even though he hadn't sunken to the depths until after she broke their engagement.

And now those lies were keeping him distant from Emma.

And yet, how could he tell her the truth now? The timing

couldn't possibly be worse. She would write him off for sure. And who could blame her.

No, right now she needed a friend, a listening ear. And that's what he would be. Even as he knew he could not let their friendship go beyond that—merely friends. Not until she knew the full truth—every detail—and could make her own decision about whether it was something she could live with. Something she could forgive.

So, if you were only going to be friends with a woman, you didn't ask her out on a date. So now what? They sort of had an understanding about going garage sale-ing together next Friday. Maybe he'd just call her tonight. See how she was doing with the whole adoption thing.

He tried to put himself in her shoes, but to be honest, he didn't think it would be that big of a deal if he found out he was adopted. He'd always felt a little like an outsider in his family anyway. Maybe because he'd come along after his brothers were older. Declan and Liam had completely different memories of their childhood than he did.

But Emma was an only child and she'd apparently been very close to her parents and at least one set of grandparents. Finding out she was adopted and had no blood relation to the people she'd thought were her family, would understandably be difficult.

He tried to think what he could do to cheer her up. Flowers had always been his go-to. He'd never met a woman yet who didn't love them. But you just didn't bring a bouquet of flowers to a flower farmer. It would be like bringing cookies to a professional baker or a cheap art print to an artist.

Artist... That was it. He made a mental note to call her on his way home from work. He thought about just surprising her at her house, but quickly decided against that. But he might just happen to be at the farmers market tomorrow.

Even so, he would tread lightly with this woman until he could prove himself worthy of her.

"THESE ARE BEAUTIFUL. YOU GREW THEM?" The middle aged woman turned the bouquet of peonies and sweet peas one way and then another, seeming genuinely impressed. She already had an armful of produce in bags from several other vendors at the farmers market.

Emma gave the woman her best smile even though she didn't feel much like smiling. "I did. The peonies don't bloom for long, but they're my favorites."

"I can see why. You have a greenhouse?"

"No. Maybe someday. Mostly I grow everything in raised beds. The soil's too sandy otherwise." She engaged with the customer, but from the corner of her eye she saw Tadhg strolling toward her booth, a large canvas portfolio-style bag slung heavily over one shoulder. Probably more pickle jars. Or he'd gotten here early this morning and already shopped the market.

"I definitely want one of these bouquets, but I'll probably stop back later," the woman was saying. She lifted the arm laden with produce bags. "I need to keep at least one arm free."

Emma laughed. "Of course. That'd be fine. If you want to go ahead and pay for it, you can choose the one you want and I'll set it back for you. I can't guarantee it will still be here otherwise…"

"Oh. That's probably a good idea." The woman picked up one small jar, then another, and finally settled on the third. She held out a twenty dollar bill.

Emma took it, marked the bouquet sold, and set it carefully underneath the table behind her. "It'll be here until five. Don't forget. You'd be surprised how often that happens."

"Oh, don't worry. I won't." The woman thanked her and moved to the next booth.

"Hey there." Tadhg slid into the spot where the woman had stood in front of Emma's booth. "How's business this morning?"

She gave a little wave. "Not bad. It usually picks up around nine. Everybody's just looking right now. They don't want to lug everything around the market all morning." Grinning, she motioned toward his bag. "Apparently you didn't get the memo? What did you buy?"

He shook his head. "Actually, I brought something for you. From home."

"For me?"

He nodded and thrust the bag at her. "If you don't have any place to store it, I can come back later."

Her curiosity got the best of her. "Can I look?"

"Of course."

She peered inside then quickly back at him. "Tadhg, no... You don't have to do this. We agreed you got first dibs." She pulled the painting from the bag and ran a hand over the frame. "Oh, the frame looks like new. Did you refinish it?"

"Just cleaned and oiled it. It was already in pretty good shape."

"Tadhg... Seriously, you didn't have to do this."

"I know I didn't *have* to, but... I was trying to think what I could do to cheer you up and..." He shrugged.

"You're so sweet." Swallowing over the lump in her throat, she took the painting from him and inspected it again, front and back. "It cleaned up so beautifully."

"It'll look great in your house."

"I know just where I'll hang it too." She eyed him. "If you're sure..."

"Of course I'm sure. I can help you hang it if you want." He pointed to the braided picture wire on the back of the painting. "I tightened this up a little, but it might need to be redone. I can do that for you too."

She'd hung many a picture in her adult life, but he didn't need to know that. "That'd be great. This was really sweet of you."

"I know."

His ornery smirk lifted her spirits as much as the painting had.

"Are you absolutely sure though? You seemed pretty smitten

with this." She hugged the painting to her chest, hoping he wouldn't change his mind.

"So did you. And I think you need it worse than I do."

She swallowed hard. "You're going to make me cry if you aren't careful."

"Would that be so bad?"

"No." She hugged the painting again. "And I do love it. Do you want to come over tonight? To help me hang it?" Her book club was meeting tonight, but she'd already planned to skip. She didn't want to risk anyone asking about her ancestry test. And this way, if anyone asked, she'd have the best excuse for why she missed —a date. At least that's how her book club friends would see it.

"Sure. Can I bring a pizza or something?"

"That would be nice. I'm never in the mood to cook after the markets."

"It's a date..." He looked away and shuffled his feet. "It's a *deal* then. Does seven o'clock sound good?"

"It does."

"Listen—" He reached for the painting. "I can take this for now and bring it back when I come tonight—so you don't have to mess with it."

She considered his offer, then pulled the painting close. "Thanks, but given its history, I think I'll just keep it right here. I'd be really mad if you were a no-show tonight."

He took a step back and affected a frown. "I can't believe you think I'd do something like that."

"Sorry..." She tried to look contrite. "That was really rude after you brought me the painting in the first place."

"Exactly!"

"All the same, I think I'll hang on to it."

Laughing, he rolled his eyes. "And no doubt it'll already be hung by the time I get there with the pizza."

"No. I promise to wait on that. But it'll be hard. I really do love this, Tadhg. More than you loved it, I think."

"Oh, don't be so sure."

She gave a soft smile, surprised again by the tears that were so near the surface. "Thank you. Seriously. I do feel better. That might be the sweetest thing anyone has ever done for me."

Maybe she was being too transparent, but it was the truth. And if she'd learned anything from the shocking thing that had happened to her, it was how very important the truth was.

She noticed a couple lingering a respectful distance behind Tadhg, waiting their turn at her booth. She looked past him and nodded to let them know she saw them.

Tadhg turned and spotted them. "Oh." Looking embarrassed, he took a step back. "Sorry, I'm keeping your customers waiting."

She gave him a grateful look. "I'll see you tonight. Thanks again. I mean it."

He mumbled an apology to the waiting couple and strolled to the next booth.

She quickly tucked the painting behind the tablecloth on her back table and greeted her customers with a smile. Genuine this time.

Chapter Thirteen

The porch lights were on when Tadhg parked in front of Emma's house. All the way over, he'd tried to figure out how he could de-escalate things with her until she was past her crisis and until he could talk to her and come clean.

But giving her the painting—while it certainly seemed to have cheered her up—had also had the effect of making her warm to him in a decidedly romantic way. This was getting complicated and he didn't know how to extricate himself from it without hurting Emma more than she'd already been hurt.

He raked his fingers through his hair—hair that desperately needed cutting. *Lord, help me find a way. Don't let me make it worse for her.*

He gathered the still-hot pizza box and climbed the steps, but before he had a chance to knock, she opened the door with a hammer and tape measure in hand.

He laughed. "Boy you don't waste any time, do you? Don't you want to eat first? Before the pizza gets cold?"

"Not really, but I guess you make a good point." She laid the tools on a small table beside the door. "Come on back to the kitchen and I'll pour our cokes. Or I have lemonade, if you'd rather."

"Lemonade sounds good."

He followed her to the kitchen and opened the pizza box. Without asking, he retrieved plates from where she'd gotten them the night she made lasagna. He already felt at home in her kitchen. In her house. "Where's Bud?"

She looked around the kitchen expectantly. "I'm not sure. Probably back in the bedroom. Don't worry, he'll come out as soon as he smells pizza."

Tadhg laughed when, a minute later, the cat sauntered into the kitchen. "Boy, you called that one."

She winced. "He knows I'm a pushover. Why do you think he's so fat?" She pinched off a small piece of sausage and knelt to offer it to the cat. "You're a spoiled rotten kitty-cat, aren't you, buddy?" she cooed.

Why did this woman have to be so stinkin' cute? She sure wasn't making it easy for him to put on the brakes.

They filled their plates and Emma poured lemonade over ice into two large tumblers. He followed her to the dining table where the view of the backyard filled the window. "It's still a little too warm on the loggia, but maybe we can go out there later."

They ate in silence for a few minutes before Tadhg broached the elephant in the room. "So, how are you feeling by now?"

"Okay, I guess. I honestly think I'm still kind of in shock."

"Who wouldn't be? I'm sorry. I wish I could make it better."

"You already did. Seriously, that was so sweet to bring me the painting."

"Even though you didn't trust me to bring it back tonight," he teased.

"It's not that I didn't trust you... I just didn't want it out of my sight. I can't wait to hang it." She pointed up at the wall behind her where several framed paintings and photos were arranged. "This is where I want to put it. I want to make kind of a gallery wall, I think. But I'll see how this looks by itself first. It's quite a bit bigger than I thought."

The painting of the lighthouse was leaning against the wall

under the hanging artwork. He didn't know much about decorating, but he wasn't a fan of gallery walls. He preferred to let one painting shine in each space. But maybe that was because there weren't any walls in his apartment big enough for a gallery. Of course, he wouldn't offer that opinion unless she asked.

They finished eating and she scooted the table away from the wall and started taking down the paintings that were there. She collected the picture hangers and nails into a little pile on the table, then held the new painting up to the wall.

"Ooh. That'll look so good there," he said. "Here... Let me hold it so you can stand back and see what you think."

She handed him the painting and went around to the other side of the table. The muddy aqua shade on the wall was the perfect background for the painting.

"Move it up about two inches."

He did, watching her expression.

"What do you think?"

"I think it would look better in my house."

"Oh, Tadhg... Honestly, if you want it, of course you can—"

"I'm just kidding, you crazy woman. I wouldn't have given it to you if I didn't mean for you to have it. I think it looks fantastic there." He leaned the painting against the wall again.

She shot him a guilty look. "It really does, doesn't it? I mean, it looks like it was made for this room."

"I hate to admit it, but it looks like it was made for this house."

Her smile was victorious. "Let's hang it then. Hold it up again and I'll mark where the hanger needs to go."

A few minutes later, they stood admiring the painting with satisfaction. There'd been no more mention of a gallery wall, and now she gathered up the smaller paintings and packed them into an Amazon box.

She tucked the box in the coat closet off the entryway and came back into the room, looking at the painting as if seeing it for the first time. "Oh! I love it! I really do, Tadhg."

"It looks good."

She clapped her hands. "Thank you so much." She approached him with her arms open for a hug. An innocent, friendly hug to show her gratitude.

But the look on her face was so sweet, so...intimate, that he panicked. He pivoted and hurried over to the painting, pretending to straighten it, even though it was already perfectly straight. When he looked back at her and dared to meet her gaze, he saw the hurt in her eyes.

Feeling as awkward as he had on his first date in high school, he bowed his head. "Um... Do you want something else to drink?"

"I can get it." Her voice went up an octave. "You want more lemonade?"

"Maybe just water this time. Thanks."

"The sun's behind the trees now. We could go out on the loggia. I—I'll bring our drinks out." It was obvious he'd made things awkward.

"Okay." He went out the door they'd used last time and instead of taking one side of the porch swing where they'd sat before, he took a lawn chair across from the swing.

She brought their drinks out and set his in front of him on the low coffee table. If she noticed his strategic seating, she didn't let on. She sat in one corner of the swing and sipped her drink.

While he racked his brain to think of something to talk about, she stopped swinging, cleared her throat, and said his name.

"Huh?"

"Did I say or do something that...I don't know...made you uncomfortable?"

"No," he lied. *Another* lie. "Why?"

She shrugged. "I don't know. It's just—" She sighed and started the swing swaying again with one foot. "I'm trying to figure you out, I guess. For somebody who tells me practically on our first date that he's looking for a wife and I seem like I might be a possibility, you sure have clammed up. I'm not saying I want us to get super serious overnight or anything. But if you've changed your mind, if you've decided I'm not a possibility any more, please just tell me. You won't hurt my feelings."

He opened his mouth to say something.

But she stopped the swing. "No, that's a lie. It *would* hurt my feelings. But not as much as you stringing me along for weeks and then dumping me. Please don't drag things out if you've already decided this isn't going to work."

Closing his eyes, he blew out a sigh. "It's not that."

He wanted to kick himself. She was already hurting over the shock of finding out she'd been lied to her whole life, and he'd managed to add to her sorrow instead of finding a way to comfort her. But nothing had changed. If he came clean about the ways he'd deceived her, it would be far worse than if he just slinked off into the sunset.

Even just telling her that he hadn't been completely honest with her about some things in his past would be making it all about him. And would feel like yet another stab in the back. The timing couldn't be worse. He either came clean with her now and added to the betrayal she was already feeling, or he told another half-truth and said everything was fine and kept pretending he'd been upfront with her from the beginning. At some point he had to be honest with her.

But neither now or later was a viable option.

He looked up to see her waiting patiently for an answer.

"What is it then?" she finally said.

"It's not you, Emma. I...I'm working on some things about myself. It honestly has nothing to do with you, except that you don't deserve to get caught in the middle while I'm trying to sort my sorry self out."

"What is it about? Can you just tell me that?"

"I just need to get right with God about some stuff." He stood and took a step backwards. "I'm really sorry. I...I like you a lot, but I need to figure some things out before things get serious with us."

She rose, hanging on to the thick rope that held the swing as if it were a lifeline. "It's not something we could figure out together?"

He shook his head. "I'm truly sorry. I feel like a jerk. You're already hurting, I know. But this is...kind of connected and I don't want to hurt you worse."

"Connected?" Her forehead furrowed. "You know something about my adoption?"

"No, no. Not connected like that. I shouldn't have said that. It's just— I don't want to add to what you're already going through."

"So, are you breaking up with me?"

"Were we official?" He gave a half smile.

Her jaw tensed. "I have no idea. You're giving such mixed signals, Tadhg. You flirt with me and act like you really like me, and then the minute I confide in you or get too close, you pull away. I have no idea," she said again.

"I know. That's my fault. Not yours. I need to work out some things. On my own."

"Is this about me being adopted? I mean, is it because you're having trouble handling what I'm going through?"

He shook his head. "No, it's not that. I understand how hard this must be for you, but I hope you don't think that what you found out changes who you are one tiny bit. I don't care what your *heritage* is, Emma. You are a beautiful person inside and out."

She was silent for a long minute. "Okay. Thank you...I guess."

"No, this is my own issue. It's not about you. I promise. I just have some...soul-searching to do."

She gave him a sideways glance. "Any idea how long this mysterious self-help project might take."

Ouch. He had that coming. But he couldn't give her an answer. Even though he'd meant what he said about not caring who her parents were, still, part of the timing depended on her. If she could overcome the feeling that she'd been betrayed, maybe she could forgive him for his deceit. He wasn't lying to himself when he believed he would have told her everything *tonight* if only she hadn't been going through her own trauma. "I don't know for sure. And I'm not asking you to wait for me. But...I hope you will."

Her chin quivered. "I'll be praying for you then. But I'm not going to wait forever. Just so you know."

"Fair enough." In some crazy way her comment gave him hope. He slipped his shoes on. "I'd better go. I can show myself out."

Looking as if he'd just struck her, she sat back down on the swing.

He was halfway to the door before he realized what he hadn't said. "I'll be praying for you, too, Emma."

Chapter Fourteen

Emma woke in a fog Sunday morning. She fed Bud, showered and went through the motions getting ready for church, but when it was time to walk out the door, she just couldn't do it.

Surprisingly, she'd fallen asleep quickly after Tadhg left her house and she'd slept well. But now she felt numb, a thousand thoughts assailing her. Tadhg had said he wasn't bothered by the things she'd learned about her history—or lack of one. But was he just saying that because, well...what else could he say?

She stopped herself. No, that didn't fit the caring, compassionate man she'd gotten to know so far. He'd said it and she would believe it. But maybe he just didn't want to deal with her being upset. Some guys hated drama and avoided it at all costs. That wasn't a very good quality for a boyfriend, and certainly not for a future husband. But that didn't sound like the Tadhg she'd come to know either.

Still, if the man she was falling in love with couldn't confide in her about something he was wrestling with, that wasn't a good way to start a relationship. Was this why Becca had broken up with him only two weeks before their wedding?

Like a hummingbird, her thoughts flitted back and forth from last night's hurtful conversation with Tadhg, to what the DNA test had revealed, to her conversations with her mom. Her first instinct was to call Mom and talk to her about everything the way they always had. But everything had changed between them. And now she didn't feel like she could talk to her about anything when she couldn't talk to her about the one thing that felt most important.

Right now, it was a moot point since Mom had texted yesterday morning—quite matter-of-factly—that she and Bill were going to Florida for a long weekend. Bill's sister lived in Destin and they often went to visit, but Emma suspected the purpose of this visit was to escape her interrogations.

If they left for more than a few days, Mom often asked her to bring in the mail and water the plants, but this was only a four-day trip and they hadn't mentioned having her stop by. But now, remembering Tadhg's question about photos of her as a baby in the hospital, an idea began to take shape.

She had a key to the house, and she knew where those photos were. The photo albums were on a bookshelf in plain sight and before everything had gone south, Mom would have gladly given her access to them. She wasn't so sure she was even welcome there now. Going while they were in Florida might be her only chance to look at the photos and get some questions answered.

Before she could talk herself out of it, she got in the car and headed for Savannah. Mom had moved into Bill's house in Georgetown after they married. Emma had never lived there, but she'd always felt welcome. Still, it was Bill's house. He had two sons several years older than Emma, and though they lived in Washington State and rarely visited, it was understood that the house would one day be theirs.

An hour and a half later, winding through the curvy Georgetown streets lined with crepe myrtles and live oaks, she started to get cold feet. Only the prospect of seeing those photos and getting some answers kept her from turning her car around and heading home.

The house was set back from the street with moss-draped oaks protecting the views from neighbors. Even so, when she saw the homeowner next-door out working in his yard, she drove on past Bill's house and circled slowly back around, waiting until the man disappeared behind his house before she turned into the driveway. She pulled up close to the garage where she wouldn't be as likely to be seen. She didn't want a neighbor mentioning to Bill or her mom that she'd been here.

She peered through the window in the garage door to make sure their car was gone and even though only Bill's work car was there, she rang the doorbell twice and waited several minutes, just in case, before letting herself in with her key.

"Mom? Anybody home?" Her voice echoed through the empty house. She walked through the rooms, checking the houseplants she usually watered, just so she could say she had in case she got caught.

That thought in itself made her feel a little sick to her stomach. To put it bluntly, she was trespassing. Maybe a small part of her *wanted* to get caught. Then maybe her mother would realize how desperate she was to know the truth about herself, the lengths she would go to know what they'd hidden from her for her entire life.

After checking the plants, she went back to the little family room where they watched TV. The photo albums were in plain sight on a bookshelf on one side of the TV console. Mom had labeled them by year and she quickly found the one for the year she'd been born. She took it to the sofa, being careful not to disturb the throw pillows and blankets arranged just-so on each end of the sofa.

She flipped through the pages to when baby Emma had first started to appear. The one she remembered of Dad holding her in what she'd thought was a hospital room was zoomed in so close that there wasn't enough background to tell for sure where they were taken. The metal arm of the chair might have been in a hospital, but it could just as easily have been a restaurant. Funny how her memory had filled in the blanks.

The first photos of her with Mom were clearly taken in the Brunswick house. There were several photos of her as a tiny baby with Nonno and Nonni at the house she lived in now. She hadn't seen these photos since she moved into the island house, and it was fascinating to see how it had changed since then. She'd almost forgotten how the place looked when her grandparents lived there.

It struck her that she didn't know if Dad's parents were even aware that she wasn't really their granddaughter. They couldn't have been more loving and warm toward her her whole life, but would it have made a difference if they'd known she shared not a drop of blood with them? If they'd known the truth, would they have willed their beloved house and property to her? It all made her feel so...*illegitimate.*

She came to the end of the album and realized that there were no photos of her with Grandma and Grandpa Baker. She thought Mom's parents had lived in Savannah her whole life, but maybe they'd moved away for a while... Or maybe they hadn't approved of her parents adopting.

Mom wasn't as close to her parents as Dad was. That's what she'd told Tadhg. It was true, but was *she* the reason why? She'd never talked to her mom about that. But in the next album, she found pictures of her with Grandma and Grandpa starting with her kindergarten graduation photos and others throughout her school years. She sat on Grandpa Baker's lap in one of them, Grandma looking adoringly at them both. Their smiles seemed sincere.

Immersed in the memories the photos evoked, her heart lurched when a clunking sound came from the front of the house. She shot off the sofa, pulse racing. Breathing hard, she stood stock still, listening. Silence. She waited a minute, then crept into the kitchen, scrambling to think what she would tell Mom and Bill if they'd come home early.

The icemaker in the fridge dumped a load of cubes into the bin, and she released a breath. Still shaky, she returned to the family room. Perusing the shelves, she retrieved the album for the year before she was born and turned the pages slowly.

She warmed at seeing her parents—Tony Fiori and Caroline Baker—as teenagers, hamming it up for the camera. They were obviously madly in love. They made a beautiful couple, Dad with his dark good looks and wavy hair, and Mom always pretty and stylish, despite her now-dated "Rachel" hairstyle that Jennifer Aniston had made famous back when her mom was young. Over the years, people had told Emma that she looked like her mother. She'd never seen the resemblance herself, but she did have Mom's honey gold hair and hazel eyes.

Mom had let her hair go gray during the pandemic, and the silver highlights looked great on her and somehow actually made her look younger than her fifty-six years. Emma had always hoped she would inherit her mother's youthful looks. But of course, that possibility was off the table now. What *would* she inherit?

She leafed through pages in the photo album, trying to figure out what month it was by the clothing and the landscapes. Some of the photos were out of order, but once she was past the Christmas photos from that year, she looked closely at what Mom was wearing. She halfway expected to see that she'd faked a pregnancy, but in each photo her mom was still slim, her stomach flat. Strange that she'd never put two and two together before.

Her phone trilled from her purse beside her, setting her heart rate off again. She checked the screen. *Mom!*

Breathing hard, she laid the phone on the sofa screen-down. She couldn't answer. Not while she was sitting in this house. She'd be forced to lie for sure. The phone kept ringing but she silenced it and forced herself to ignore it, hoping there wasn't an emergency. After a few minutes, she let herself check for a voicemail.

Nothing.

Calmer now, she looked through the albums again, getting

lost in the memories that rolled over her, yet not gaining any new insight into what had happened in the days leading up to her birth. It still puzzled her that her parents had chosen to keep her adoption a secret from her. It made her feel...*guilty* somehow. As if there was some shameful secret attached to her birth.

She looked closely at her parents' pixelated faces, trying to detect whether there was stress or sadness there, but she couldn't make their expressions appear as anything but delighted and in love—with each other and with her. There was a measure of comfort in that. And it reminded her of the things Mom had told her: *Your dad and I loved you from the second we laid eyes on you. We loved you more than life itself...*

There was no reason not to believe that. So why would they perpetrate a lie that they'd intended to carry through their entire lives?

She had her birth certificate with Mom's and Dad's names on it. But there had to be adoption records somewhere—and a birth certificate with her birth parents' names on it. Her research said the state of Georgia required that, and then a new, amended birth certificate was issued that listed the adoptive parents. That was the one she had, and according to the websites she'd studied, in Georgia at least, that amended certificate was good for anything legal she needed a birth certificate for.

But would Mom have the original? Probably not if it was sealed and if she'd never intended to tell Emma the truth. But she didn't think her mom was the type to keep things in a bank safe deposit box, so if she had a copy of the original certificate, it was likely in this house somewhere.

But where? She wouldn't feel right snooping in Mom's personal banking or legal papers, but this was *her* life. It wasn't snooping if it was her own records, was it? She was an adult. She had a right to know her own history.

Mom shared office space with Bill in a small bedroom at the end of the hall. She would have felt better if Bill's desk hadn't been in that room, but after checking the driveway and the garage for their car, she went down the hallway and sat at her mom's desk. She opened the top drawer to see neatly organized office supplies—paper clips, rubber bands, extra keys, envelopes... She smiled. Mom's desk drawer was almost identical to Emma's in her little office alcove. Dad had always accused the two of them of being neat freaks. She'd definitely come by her tidy, organized ways honestly and—

Come by them honestly. The phrase stopped her. No, there was nothing honest about this whole mess. She'd *learned* things from her mom, of course. But tidiness wasn't necessarily in her DNA. And if it was, it wasn't from Mom.

The drawers on the left side held old bank statements, insurance policies, and a folder for bills—all neatly stacked or filed in each space.

She reached for the file cabinet drawer on the right, but it resisted her pull. She scooted back and inspected the drawer handle and noticed the keyhole at the top. The drawer was locked.

That had to mean something, didn't it? Remembering the small collection of keys in the top drawer, she searched for one that would fit. She located it quickly and before her conscience could stop her, she unlocked the drawer and slid it open.

A dozen or more olive green legal file folders hung in a neat row, each one bearing a label printed in Mom's precise handwriting. Emma slid from her chair and knelt in front of the drawer so she could read the labels without touching them.

Household Receipts, Life Insurance, Medical Records, Will & Trust, Baker Estate, E. Fiori...

Seeing her name on a label toward the back of the drawer, she took in a sharp breath. That was her. She was the only E. Fiori she knew. Why hadn't Mom just written Emma?

But this had to be it. Heart in her throat, she memorized where the file went among the others and lifted it out, clutching it to her chest. Did she really want to know what this folder held?

The doorbell rang and she nearly jumped out of her skin. Dropping the folder back where she'd gotten it, she quietly closed the drawer and tiptoed into the guest room across the hall where she could look out on the driveway.

She cautiously lifted one slat of the plantation blind that covered the window. Her car was where she'd left it, but it was the only vehicle on the drive. The doorbell rang again and she dropped the slat and flattened herself against the wall. She felt like a common thief.

Hearing footsteps on the driveway, she lifted the slat of the blinds again. The same neighbor she'd seen in the yard next door earlier walked away and then over to his yard.

Did Bill let the neighbors know when they were going to be gone? He'd talked about getting a doorbell camera, but theirs was a safe neighborhood and Mom had talked him out of it. Emma had never had anyone question her whenever she came to pick up mail and water the plants. But the neighbor would have seen the Glynn County tags on her car and might mention it to Bill and her mom. She'd have to come up with a plausible story.

She went back to the drawer and took out the file labeled *E. Fiori*. She took a deep breath and opened the folder.

It was empty.

Chapter Fifteen

Tadhg shifted in the uncomfortable pew and tried to focus on what Pastor Shelton was saying. But it was no use. He looked at the back of the bulletin where the sermon outline was followed by blank space for taking notes.

So far, he'd written one word on the page. DILEMMA. It was a word the pastor had used in his message, but Tadhg didn't think that was why he'd written it down. He had a dilemma. One he could not see a solution to. He traced the letters again, giving up on getting anything out of the sermon.

Hmmm... d-i-l-E-M-M-A. Interesting that the word had *her* name in it. Was that supposed to be some kind of sign?

He sensed a subtle shift around him and realized Pastor Shelton was praying. Not wanting to have to talk to anyone, Tadhg slipped out of the pew and walked to the parking lot, nodding at the security guy disguised as a greeter at the church's front door.

He drove through for a foot-long sandwich at Subway, and when he pulled into the driveway, Izzy was watering flowers in the front yard. He parked in his usual place, grabbed the bag with his sandwich, and walked around to the front of the house.

"Good morning, honey," Izzy said when she saw him. "Good boy... You've been to church."

"How did you know that?"

"I can tell."

He laughed, but wondered what the giveaway was. It wasn't like he was toting a huge Bible or anything.

"Have you had lunch yet?" He held up the Subway bag, thankful he'd had them wrap the two halves of his foot-long separately. "I have plenty to share."

"Oh, goodness, no. You don't have to do that."

"I know I don't have to, but what if I wanted to?"

"Well, that would be very nice. How about if I add some of my fruit compote and some sweet tea to the mix?"

"That sounds great." He didn't know what fruit compote was, but Izzy had yet to serve him anything he didn't like.

"Do you want to come inside? Or we could sit on the porch if it's not too hot. I can turn on the ceiling fan."

"Perfect."

She flipped the switch that started the fan whirring and disappeared inside the house. She returned a few minutes later with two small plates and a fancy bowl of what looked like the canned fruit cocktail his mom used to serve with her Sunday casseroles. While Izzy went back for glasses of iced tea, Tadhg laid the sandwiches on the little metal table, placing them on napkins the girl at the drive-thru had tucked in the bag.

Izzy returned and settled into the chair opposite him. They ate in comfortable silence, and Tadhg found himself wishing Emma was here with them. She would love Izzy. And maybe she'd understand why he'd called her his grandma. But maybe that was all wishful thinking. As much as he wanted them to, he wasn't sure things were even going to work out with Emma.

When he was on his second slice of peach pie with ice cream, Izzy threw a knowing smile across the table. "So, are you going to tell me what's troubling you, young man?"

He swallowed a peach without chewing and wiped his mouth, taken aback. "Why... What makes you ask that?"

"*I've* earned these ridges in my forehead..." She tapped her forehead and then reached across the table and gently tapped his forehead in the same manner. "You are far too young to be wearing them."

He dipped his head and offered her a sheepish smile. "I guess you could say it's girl trouble."

"Uh-oh. What's her name?" She waited, watching him.

"Emma." He took a slug of iced tea and tried to think how to explain it without revealing too much. "She's a girl I've been seeing. But I'm not sure it's going to work out."

"Why is that...if you'll humor a snoopy old lady."

He laughed. "She's going through some stuff right now." He gave Izzy a shortened version of the DNA test story.

"And what does that have to do with you."

He swallowed hard. "I think she's feeling really betrayed and—" He stopped, not sure he wanted to go into details. But the kindness on Izzy's face coerced him. "The truth is, I haven't told her everything about me—my past—and now I'm afraid it's going to feel like another betrayal once she finds out. I didn't intend to keep anything from her, but we were just getting to know each other, you know?"

Izzy nodded. "Do you like her?"

"A lot."

"And you think she likes you?"

"She does now, but once she knows everything about me, maybe not so much. I don't want to lay everything on her when she's already going through some hard stuff, but if I don't tell her soon, it's going to feel like I...*lied* or something."

"*Did* you lie?"

"Not really." Feeling like Izzy could see right through him, he backpedaled. "But I guess I might have let her assume things that aren't true. I didn't think she was ready to know the whole truth, and now if I tell her the whole truth, she's gonna say 'forget you.'"

"Don't you think she should be the one to decide about that?"

He gave a shrug. "Maybe."

"Can you maybe warn her that there's something you haven't told her but let *her* decide when she's ready to hear it?"

"Maybe."

"I suppose it depends on how bad it is...what you have to tell her, I mean."

"It's pretty bad. And she knows some of it. But I kind of... downplayed the worst of it."

"You mean about you being in jail?"

He stared at her, startled. "You know that?"

Izzy looked perplexed. "Tadhg, you told me that the first time you looked at the apartment."

"I did?"

"You said, 'You'll probably need to do a background check on me so I want to be upfront.'"

"Wow. I don't remember that." He truly didn't.

"Yes, and I admit it gave me pause, but I appreciated your honesty. And I'm not sorry I said yes. You've been a good renter."

"Well, thanks. Maybe you can be my reference if she asks for one."

"Sure, but why don't you let this girl—Emma—make her own decision once she knows the truth?"

Izzy made it seem so simple. But marriage—because he *had* told Emma that was his end game—was a very different animal than renting an apartment to somebody you'd rarely see.

He wasn't ready to tell Izzy all that, but she'd given him a glimmer of hope.

"Don't be too upset if she needs a little space. She probably needs some time to figure things out given the shock she's had."

He nodded. "Yeah, probably."

"Maybe you could send her a card or send a message on your phone or whatever it is you young people do these days." She wiped the corners of her mouth on the napkin. "But don't give up too soon. Give the girl a chance."

Tadhg wasn't sure how much stock he could put in an old woman's advice, but Izzy had been Emma's age herself once upon a time—and she'd known a long and loving marriage, the kind Tadhg wanted for himself someday. He trusted Izzy's advice.

Now he just needed to figure out *how* to tell Emma the things he needed to tell her. And *when*. The one thing he did know was *why*: He was falling in love with her. And he didn't want to lose her.

EMMA SLUMPED into the desk chair and stared at the empty file folder. Mom wouldn't have created a folder unless there was something to put in it. So when had she emptied it? And where were the documents that had been in here? Had she destroyed them?

She looked at the neatly printed label. It was strange that Mom hadn't simply labeled it "Emma." As far as she knew, there were no other E. Fioris in the family, but now she wondered what other family secrets had been kept from her.

Remembering the file in front of hers labeled Baker Estate, she retrieved it from the drawer. She searched for a similar file for her Fiori grandparents and for her dad, but there were no folders marked with their names.

Opening the Baker file on the desk, she riffled through the documents it held: Papers for the sale of their home dated six months after Grandma and Grandpa had died, and birth and death certificates for both of them. She noticed both were marked as Covid-19 deaths—not as the immediate cause, but Covid-19 was listed as an "underlying cause." Seeing the name of the funeral home—a crematorium—brought back memories of her grandparents' deaths. Because of the pandemic, there had been no funeral service for either of them, but a few days after Grandpa passed away, she and Mom had gone to the cemetery and watched as the boxes holding her grandparents' ashes were buried together in one small plot.

She remembered how stoic Mom had been, especially compared to when Nonno Fiori died. Emma had been in high school then, and Nonno's funeral was the first she'd ever attended. Dad had been silent and sad-looking, but Mom wept like a baby. Understandably, she'd been inconsolable at Dad's funeral a few years later. And at Nonni's service a few years after that. At the time, Emma guessed Mom was reliving Dad's funeral as she was herself.

But remembering how unemotional Mom had been at her own parents' graveside, Emma wondered. She'd assumed Mom had just weathered so many deaths, that she was beyond emotion. But now she contemplated why Mom had never spoken about the reasons they'd always seemed closer to Dad's parents. She'd assumed it was physical distance, but it was only an hour and a half, and now that Mom lived the same distance away, Emma knew there must have been something deeper than that. Maybe that was something Mom would talk to her about.

But did it even matter now? Those hadn't been her real grandparents. Not for the first time, she wondered if her adoption was the reason for the estrangement. Maybe estrangement was too strong a word. It wasn't like they'd never spent time with her Baker grandparents. But it definitely wasn't the same as with Nonno and Nonni. Dad's parents had felt like an extension of her immediate family. It was why she'd always related so deeply to her Italian heritage.

She gave a humorless laugh and the sound of her own voice startled her. She turned over her phone and checked the time. Mom had said she and Bill wouldn't be home until tomorrow, but what if they decided to come home early?

She turned back to the file with mom's parents' information. There didn't seem to be anything unusual in Grandma and

Grandpa Baker's papers. She was admittedly surprised that Mom —who took pride in her minimalist organization—had held onto so many of her parents' papers. There were receipts for repairs on their house, property tax statements, and even receipts for small kitchen appliances. Why would Mom have kept those? Of course, all of Nonno and Nonni's paperwork for their house was in a similar folder in Emma's house. Since she'd inherited the house and moved in, she'd rarely needed to look through those papers. For all she knew, there were similar receipts in her folder.

Still, unlike her mother, she wasn't nearly as organized, and she hadn't moved twice like Mom had. She looked through the folder again, careful to keep things in the order she'd found them. A thick envelope at the back of the file held medical records. She might have been interested in those if she'd actually been their granddaughter by birth, but they meant nothing to her now. But she supposed it made sense that Mom had kept them in case *she* needed to know her own medical history. Too bad the daughter she'd adopted didn't have the same privilege.

The thought brought anger all over again. If, years down the road, she became ill and Mom wasn't around, she would be flying blind to help doctors figure out her health history. Her mom had said there wasn't anything serious in her medical ancestry, but since her birth mother had apparently died young, how could they know that? And what about her birth father. Had they bothered to ask about his history when they were making the deal to adopt her.

Making the deal. It sounded so clinical and heartless.

She rose and went down the hall to use the bathroom. The room had access from the hallway, so Mom always referred to it as the guest bath, but it served the primary bedroom as well. The door that led through to Mom and Bill's bedroom was closed, as usual. She was tempted to search there—maybe in Mom's night-stand—but that felt like too great a violation.

Washing her hands, she stared at her reflection in the mirror. *Look at you, talking about violations with everything you've already done.* She pushed away the thought, and on a whim, opened the medicine cabinet behind the mirror.

Careful not to touch anything, she did a quick inventory of the cabinet's contents. Nothing unusual, but a pill bottle from a local pharmacy caught her eye. She assumed it was Bill's but a closer look revealed her mom's name on the label. She hadn't known Mom was on any medications. She turned the bottle gingerly until she could read the name. *Amlodipine 10 MG. No refills. Doctor must authorize.*

What was Amlodipine? There was nothing on the bottle that told what it had been prescribed for. She started to enter the name into her phone, but before she finished typing, her phone vibrated in her hand. She turned it over to see Mom's photo. Why was she calling again? Heart pounding, she shut the medicine cabinet quietly and ran down the hall to the office. She quickly stuffed the papers back in the file, being careful to return the folder to where she'd found it in the drawer.

Placing the key to the file drawer in the middle of the desk so she wouldn't forget to lock it, she picked up her still-ringing phone, blew out a breath and clicked Accept.

"Hey, Mom." Too late, she realized her cheery nothing-is-wrong-in-the-world voice was not the right tone.

Sure enough, Mom instantly sounded suspicious. "Emma? Where are you?"

"Home," she lied. "I was...out in the garden. Sorry, I didn't have my phone with me." It scared her a little how easily she spun the lies.

"Where are you now?"

Something was going on. "Is everything okay?" She was truly worried now.

"Apparently not."

"What do you mean?" Muting the phone, she locked the desk drawer, pushed the chair into its place under the desk, and started gathering her things.

"You are *not* at home." Mom's voice sounded like it was coming through closed teeth.

"What...what do you mean?"

"Bill and I have been sitting on your loggia for the last hour waiting for you to get home. I can assure you that you were not working in the garden. What is going on? Where are you?"

Chapter Sixteen

"You're there? At my house? *Now?*" Emma's heart pounded harder and harder in her chest until she was sure her mom could hear it across the miles.

"Yes, we're here. Why did you tell me you were home? And where *are* you?"

"I had...some errands to run. I meant I'm on my *way* home." Holding her phone to her shoulder with her cheek, she quickly gathered her purse and surveyed the office, making sure there was no trace that she'd been here.

"Emma, you said you were in the garden."

"Oh... I was. Earlier. I'm driving home now." She hated herself for the lies.

"Okay," Mom said. "We'll wait."

"Um... You'll be waiting a while." She gave an awkward laugh. "I'm in Brunswick...almost. And I still have another stop to make. But why are you at my house? I thought you were in Florida."

"We decided to come home early. Bill and I got to talking on the drive, and we just thought we should come and...talk to you."

"I'm sorry. I don't want to make you wait." She was dying to know what they wanted to talk to her about. Maybe Mom was finally going to give her some answers. But she needed time. To compose herself. And to come up with a plausible story to explain why she'd lied. "Can we...do it another time?"

Mom blew out an audible breath. "I guess so. How soon could you get here?"

"I'm sorry, but it'll be at least an hour." Her mother was so insistent, and curiosity was eating Emma alive, but she was an hour and a half from home—if she didn't hit any traffic. She could not tell her mother that. "I've got this...other errand still. Sorry."

She felt sick to her stomach at the ease with which the lies were flowing out of her mouth. She and her mom had never had that kind of relationship and— The thought stopped her cold. What a joke. Their relationship had been one huge lie from the moment she was born. She shouldn't have to feel guilty for her little white lies. Maybe giving her mother a tiny taste of her own medicine would make her realize how her lies had made Emma feel.

"Well, I guess we'll have to talk another time. But we really would like to see you as soon as possible."

She bit her tongue. She wouldn't give her mom the satisfaction of knowing how curious she was. "I have a wedding next weekend so things will be a little crazy getting ready for that. Earlier in the week would be best."

"Could I help you with the flowers?"

"Thanks, but...you don't need to do that."

"I wouldn't mind, Emma." Mom sounded like she was near tears.

"What does Bill want to talk to me about?" She walked through the house to the garage, checking each room she'd been in to be sure there was no sign of her presence.

"It's not just him. I...I wanted him to be there when you and I talk."

"Why? So I don't beat you up?"

Stunned silence on her mom's end. Finally she said, "Emma.

Don't be ridiculous. I just wanted to have Bill here for moral support. This isn't easy for me and—"

"And you think it's easy for *me*?" She reached for the door, and the grandfather clock in the living room chose that moment to start chiming the hour. She jabbed at the Mute button on her phone.

"Emma? What was that?"

Pulse hammering, she quickly locked the door and closed it behind her. As she ran for her car, she unmuted her phone. "Sorry... You cut out for a minute. I'll text you when I get home and we can figure out a time to get together."

She hit End on the phone and turned to Bill. "She's not coming. Apparently her errands are more important. She is lying about where she is. She's never lied to me. At least I don't think she has."

"I'm sorry, Caroline. We need to give her a little grace."

She shook her head. Maybe he was right, but in this moment she felt nothing but deep disappointment. She leaned back against the swing and looked out over the lush gardens Emma had nurtured here at Tony's parents' house. This place always carried with it memories of him. A little confusing, when Bill sat here beside her on the swing, one arm around her trembling shoulders, concern etching his handsome face. She'd given two men her heart, and that always felt a little treacherous. Even though she knew in her heart that she'd loved them both equally and purely.

She'd betrayed neither. But had she betrayed Emma? Her daughter felt she'd been lied to, and she knew she'd have felt the same in Emma's shoes. She still couldn't believe Emma had let herself into their house and no doubt rifled through personal files in the desk she shared with Bill. But she knew the sound of that clock, and at the first chime, she instantly knew what her daughter had done. It was a betrayal. Not just to her, but to Bill too—it was his house after all.

She'd long ago hidden away or destroyed anything that might give away her secrets, but not because she'd ever dreamed her daughter would breach her trust this way. She'd done it so that someday when she was gone, Emma wouldn't find out the cruel truth.

DRIVING HOME, Emma felt like she'd murdered someone. She wasn't a liar. Never had been. She'd always valued honesty above all virtues. So what did it say about her that she could deceive her mom—the very person she was closest to—with such ease?

She felt like crying, but the tears wouldn't come. All she felt was an icy, dull paralysis.

Was this how Mom had felt keeping her own awful secret? Or if you told a lie for long enough, did it start to numb the guilt? She didn't want to have to find out the answer to that question.

Her phone rang again and she almost ignored it, thinking it would be her mom. But it was Tadhg. He was the one bright spot in her life...even if things were sometimes confusing where he was concerned.

"Hello?"

"Hey there. Are you busy?"

"I'm driving. On my way home. What are you up to?"

"There's something I need to talk to you about."

"You sound...serious."

"It is kind of serious. Nobody's dead or anything." He gave a humorless laugh. "I know you've got some heavy things going on, but I don't want to let this go too long before I talk to you about it."

"Okay... Were you wanting to talk now?"

"Would you care if I came over? Or maybe we could meet somewhere?"

"Tonight?"

"If that's okay."

Curiosity got the best of her again. "Can you give me a hint?"

"I just want to set the record straight on some things I told you—or I guess things I didn't tell you is more like it."

Great. More lies. More dishonesty. She sighed into the phone. "This really isn't a good time, Tadhg. I just had a hard conversation with my mom. I honestly don't know if I have the bandwidth for anything else."

"I'm sorry. And I understand...of course. It can wait. Is there a good night this week? Or maybe we could do breakfast before work some morning?"

"I have to do flowers for a wedding this weekend. I—" The words came out almost against her will. They were words of self-preservation, self-defense. And she knew she needed to say them, even though a part of her felt like she might be pushing away the best thing that had ever happened to her.

She wanted to say yes so badly. Wanted to see his face, hold his hand, pour out everything to him. Instead, she heard her own answer as if someone else was speaking. "This just really isn't a good time. In my life. I like you, Tadhg... I really do. But I have to work some things out in my own life before I'm...healthy enough to be in a relationship."

And that, at least, was true.

She waited, hearing only silence on his end. It reminded her too much of her mom's silence a few minutes ago. She was pushing away everyone she cared about.

"Wow," he said finally. "Is this you giving me a taste of my own medicine?"

"What do you mean?"

"Are you...breaking up with me? Because I backed away from you?"

"I wasn't aware there was anything to break up." *What is wrong with you, Fiori? Are you* trying *to destroy every relationship you care about?*

"Okay then... I guess I have my answer."

She wanted to cry. He sounded so hurt. And taken aback.

"Tadhg, wait... I'm sorry." She waited for what seemed an eternity. "Tadhg? I'm sorry. Yes, please... Let's have breakfast. Tomorrow maybe?"

She waited. But it was too late. He'd hung up.

Tadhg laid his phone on the kitchen table and stared at the screen. Gloom settled over him in a way that was frighteningly familiar and brought memories crashing back of the days after Becca had broken their engagement.

At least this time, he wasn't even tempted to drown his sorrows in alcohol or fist fights or even the pain of a tattoo. He rubbed the tiger on his arm, grateful for that realization. He tucked his phone back into his pocket and opened the fridge in search of supper, despite not being in the least hungry now.

Show me what to do, God. You know how I feel about that woman. But I won't chase after her without Your clear leading. Give me patience and show me what to do in the meantime.

He was still praying, asking God for wisdom, when his phone rang. He slipped it from his pocket, hoping it was Emma. Man, it would be nice if God answered that quickly every time he prayed.

But instead, his brother's face smiled back from the screen.

He answered with a sincere apology. "Liam! Hey man. Sorry I never got back to you. What's up?"

"Well, I don't mean to bug you, but Kacey says I should, so you can blame her. We'd really like to come down and see you this summer. We're wanting the kids to get a taste of what my summers were like when I was their age. Think you could make that work?"

"Yeah. Sure...come on down. I don't have room to put you up in my apartment, but there's—"

"Oh, no, man. We've got an Airbnb reserved. Kacey's a big fan of those. We just wanted to make sure you weren't going to be out of town or anything."

"So, when were you thinking?" As if his social calendar was overflowing.

"Well, I know this is really short notice, but a friend of Kacey's is getting married on the island Saturday. If that's not too late of notice we'd love to hang out Friday. The wedding is Saturday night, but we'd probably try to get there Thursday night and hang out with you Friday and Saturday until the wedding. Any chance you can get off work Friday?"

"Oh, man... We've been swamped and we have a guy out sick this week. But I might be able to take the afternoon off." Mild panic rose in him at the thought of seeing his brother again, but he'd just as soon get it over with. And maybe *this* was God's answer to the prayer he'd just prayed. "I'll do my best to get off early," he said before he could come up with an excuse. "What do you guys want to do while you're here?"

"All the usual things. I want to give the kids a taste of what my childhood vacations were like. The beach, of course, and we want to rent bikes and ride around the island."

"Sure. Yeah, there's a great trail there."

"Oh, I remember. Don't you?"

"I remember the boardwalk on the beach, but I'm not sure I ever rode bikes with Mom and Dad there. Do you want me to reserve bikes or anything?"

"No, you don't need to do that. We can play that by ear. Mostly we just want to hang out with you and...catch up."

"Sure. That'll be great. This'll make Mom happy." He gave an awkward laugh.

Liam chuckled. "I haven't told her yet. I didn't want to get her hopes up in case you were busy."

"Nah, I'm not busy. It'll be good to see you guys. Remind me how old the kids are now."

"Ethan's nine and Amelia is almost six."

"What? When did that happen." Ethan had been a little kid and his niece hadn't even started walking when he moved to the island. He'd been home a couple times since then, but he still pictured Liam's kids as toddlers.

"Yeah, tell me about it." Liam snorted. "I'm an old man, bro."

"Shoot, you were an old man when I was born."

"Watch it, buddy. I can still take you."

"We'll see about that." He felt better already, and at least his brother's visit would give him something to do instead of sitting home feeling sorry for himself. "Well, hey, text me when you know your schedule. But I'll keep the weekend open. And Friday afternoon if you can get here early. Are you driving?"

"Yeah. Pray for me."

Tadhg laughed, remembering family vacations in the car with his big brothers fighting across the backseat with him caught in the middle. "Will do."

"Okay then, we'll see you this coming weekend. Kacey will be glad."

"Tell her thanks for making you call. And sorry I never got around to it. Oh, and let me tell Mom, okay? I never have anything good to tell her."

His brother laughed. "If Kacey hasn't already called her. See you soon, bro."

Tadhg was still smiling when the line went dead. And before he could come up with an excuse, he dialed his mom.

Chapter Seventeen

"Emma?"

"Mom. Hi." She tucked her phone between her shoulder and her cheek and dried her hands on a dish towel. She hated this awkwardness between them, and her actions yesterday had only made that worse.

"Bill and I are on our way over. Will you be home for a few minutes?" This had to be about Mom catching her in a lie yesterday.

"Like I said, I have a wedding this weekend, so things are going to be a little crazy here, but yes, I'm home this morning."

"This won't take long. We'll be there in about thirty-five minutes.

"Oh. Okay." She glanced at the clock. It was after eight, they would have already eaten breakfast, but she offered anyway. "I can make eggs and toast."

"No, we ate before we left."

"I'll make coffee then."

"No, don't do that. We won't be staying long."

"Okay..."

Her mother was acting very strange. And it was unusual that Bill was coming with her. Suddenly remembering the prescription she'd found in the medicine cabinet, a sick feeling came over her. She never had finished looking up the name of the medication. And now she couldn't remember it. She thought it started with an A. She opened the browser on her phone and looked for the window she'd opened. She'd typed *A-M* but nothing more.

She googled "medicines that start with AM." A long list loaded. There must have been close to two hundred names and none of them looked familiar. It was probably nothing. Older people took medications. It didn't necessarily mean anything. And she couldn't ask her mom about it without raising worse suspicions. No, more accurately, she'd forfeited the right to ask.

While she waited for them to arrive, growing more nervous by the minute, she cleaned the litter box, watered her houseplants, and started a pot of coffee, just in case.

Looking out through the loggia to the gardens, she cringed at how much work she had to do to get ready for Saturday's wedding. There was a good selection of flowers blooming, but the bride had requested a certain peach colored rose in her bridal bouquet that Emma didn't grow, so she needed to pick those up from a florist in town. But before then, there was weeding and mowing and watering, since there was no rain in the forecast as of this morning.

Exactly thirty-five minutes from when she'd hung up from talking to Mom, she heard a car on the driveway out front. She went to the door, but feeling suddenly on edge, instead of going out to greet them, she watched from behind the curtain and waited for them to ring the doorbell.

Her nerves calmed a little when Mom and Bill both gave her their usual greeting hugs, but her mother was barely seated on the sofa when she locked eyes with Emma and came right to the point.

"Why did you lie to us?"

She should have expected this question, but for some crazy reason, she hadn't. She played dumb. "What do you mean?"

"Emma. You know what I mean. Why did you tell me you

were here at the house yesterday, working in the garden, when you clearly were not?"

She swallowed hard. "I'm sorry. I shouldn't have done that. I was wrong." She felt genuinely remorseful, but maybe not for the right reasons. If she was honest with herself, she was mostly sorry she'd gotten caught.

"So, where *were* you when we called?"

"I told you... I was running errands."

"Where?" Her mother knew something.

"Why are you...interrogating me?"

"Emma." The expression on her mom's face was one she hadn't seen since she was a teenager. Frustration, anger...

Bill put a hand on her knee as if to settle her down.

Mom shot him a warning look and turned back to Emma. "I'm going to ask you a question and I want the truth. Why were you in our house yesterday? You knew we were gone."

Emma's mind raced. She wanted to make an excuse. Say she'd thought she was supposed to water the plants. But that wouldn't fool her mom. She was caught. And she was in the wrong. How had she let things go this far? And yet something kicked her into survival mode, and instead of coming clean, telling the truth, asking forgiveness—all the things she knew she needed to do—she lashed out at Mom. "You want the truth?" She glared at her mother. "Well, so do I. How about if you tell *me* the truth, I'll do the same."

Mom sniffed and lowered her head, trembling.

Bill put his arm around her and gave Emma a hard look. "Emma, your mother is a woman of honor and trustworthiness. She keeps the promises she makes no matter what. It is killing her to have this rift between you, but you are asking her to betray who she is."

Something about the way Bill defended Mom made Emma jealous of the closeness they shared. But just as quickly, anger rushed through her. "Listen to yourself. Betray who she is? What about who *I* am? I don't even know the answer to that. And now it sounds like I never will."

Against her will, tears came and she continued through sobs. "This is killing me too. I hate it. But what am I supposed to do? I can't just get over it. She lied to me. Both of them did. Mom and Dad. My whole life. How can a parent do that?" She spoke about Mom as if she wasn't in the room.

"I know that must hurt," Bill said, his voice gentle. "But Emma, you know Caroline—your mom. You know her. She loves you. She would never intentionally do anything to hurt you. But neither is she going to break a promise she made to some people who were very precious to her—"

"Precious because—" Mom sat up and patted Bill's knee, seeming to gather new strength. "Precious because we have you because of that promise I made. Emma, I'm not going to make accusations, but Bill and I know that you were at our house yesterday."

"But how did you—?"

"That doesn't matter. What matters is that you breached our trust. Just so you know, there is nothing in our house—Bill's and mine—that will answer your questions."

Bill rose and paced behind the sofa. His lips moved silently, and Emma thought he was praying. It touched her, even as it scared her a little.

Even so, she turned her pleas on him. "Do *you* know, Bill? Do you know my story? Because I sure don't."

He started to open his mouth, but Mom interrupted. "Leave Bill out of this, Emma. I have told you everything I possibly can. I have assured you that you don't have anything in your health history to worry about. I've expressed in every way I know how, that your dad and I loved you since the moment you were placed in our arms. You couldn't have grown up in a more loving, caring home, surrounded by grandparents and friends who loved you and treated you with kindness. You've been blessed with an inheritance that has allowed you to live out your passion and not worry about money. And frankly, you're acting like a spoiled, ungrateful —" Her voice broke on the word.

Emma felt a pang of conviction. Everything her mom said was true. And she *was* grateful, but that didn't change the fact that she kept reliving memories from what she thought had been a happy childhood, and now every one of them felt tainted with the colossal lie she'd grown up with. And worse, it was turning *her* into a liar.

Mom rose from the sofa, looking suddenly older. She held out a hand, palm up. "I'd like to have our keys back, please. The keys to our house."

Feeling gutted, she went to get her purse, dug out the keys, and put them in her mother's hand. "I'm sorry. I…shouldn't have done that."

"I forgive you. And I love you. But I think this is going to take some time for you—for both of us—to come to terms with things. I've told you everything I can. Until you can accept that, I don't think—" Her voice wavered again. "I think it might be best if we take some time away from each other."

"Mom? Are you serious?" She couldn't believe this was happening. "What do you mean, time away?"

"I just think we shouldn't see each other for a while. I don't know what else to do, Emma. You leave me no choice." She swiped at her eyes and motioned to Bill. "We need to go."

He followed her to the door, but gave Emma a sympathetic shrug as he passed.

She stared at the door long after it closed behind them. And somehow she knew better than to dare hope Mom might come back and ask for the same forgiveness she'd offered Emma.

Numb with disbelief, she changed clothes and went to the garden. What kind of promise could Mom have possibly made that compelled her to make a sham of their relationship? It made no sense. The truth behind her birth must be beyond awful.

Chapter Eighteen

Tadhg surveyed his apartment, wishing for the dozenth time that he hadn't offered to make supper for Liam and his family. They could just as easily have met at a restaurant somewhere. He would have happily paid—and it might well have been cheaper than the roast simmering in the crockpot. But he was a decent cook, and the savory aroma wafting through the kitchen masked any funky smells his quick cleaning spree might have missed. Plus, if he was lucky he'd have leftovers for a week, so he supposed it was a good tradeoff for the nerves that had him on edge now.

He didn't know Kacey that well, but he was sure he forgot to clean things she would zero in on and he'd probably cleaned things she wouldn't even notice. At least the toilet was sparkling. He knew enough to be sure that was taken care of.

He'd kept dinner simple—roast beef with potatoes and carrots, store-bought dinner rolls, strawberries and blueberries for the kids, and ice cream for dessert. He would have liked to make a nice cheesecake like the one Emma had served him, but he had no clue if that was an easy dessert or a hard one. He'd almost used the occasion as an excuse to call and ask her advice, but given that he kept hearing her last words to him—*I wasn't aware there was anything to break up*—he promised himself to leave her alone. At least this way, he didn't have to figure out how to introduce her to his brother. Although Liam would no doubt ask if he had a girlfriend.

He heard a car on the gravel drive and watched out the open window as the family of four spilled out of the minivan and the kids ran to climb the steep steps to his apartment.

"Amelia, be careful on the steps!" Kacey called. "Gosh, I'd hate to carry groceries up these stairs," she told Liam over her shoulder.

"It's not like he's buying groceries for a family of four." Liam brought up the rear, and before he was halfway up, the doorbell rang repeatedly.

"Ethan," Kacey hissed, "One time is plenty."

Taking a deep breath, Tadhg pasted on a smile and opened the door. "Hey guys, come on in."

"Hi, Uncle Tiger." Kacey's pint-sized mini-me, who looked nothing like Tadhg remembered, tossed him a coy look. "Dad said I can call you that."

"Your dad is right." He put up a hand for a high-five and then wondered if that was a thing for little girls. Apparently not since she backed away and hugged her mom's knees.

"Can I see your Tiger?" Ethan pointed to his arm.

"Kids, kids, give Uncle Tadhg some space. Good grief." Kacey opened her arms for a hug. "Sorry, Tadhg. They've talked about nothing but that tiger on your bicep since we told them we were coming."

He laughed. "That's funny they even remember."

"Oh, it's memorable all right," Liam said.

Tadhg bent closer to the kids and slowly scooched his sleeve up to reveal the tattoo, then cracked up when they both reacted with O-shaped mouths.

Laughing with him, his brother ducked under the doorframe and they exchanged claps on the back. "How's it going, bro? Nice place you've got here."

"It really is." Kacey sounded surprised. "And something smells amazing."

"Let's hope it tastes amazing. Are you hungry?"

"Starving!" Ethan shouted.

"Ethan. Manners!" Kacey shook the boy's shoulders affectionately, then turned to Tadhg. "What can I do to help?"

The nerves left him, and Tadhg felt his heart grow lighter. Why had he waited so long to make a reunion happen? After giving them the thirty-second tour of his apartment and getting out some decks of cards for the kids to play with, he led his sister-in-law to the kitchen.

He pulled the potatoes out of the oven and got the berries from the fridge. "Everything is pretty much ready. You can dish up your kids' plates and we'll just serve ourselves buffet-style."

"Perfect," she said.

His niece and nephew sat at the tiny kitchen table and he and Liam and Kacey gathered around the coffee table. It was nice, and Tadhg wished the rest of his family could be here. Start new traditions together. But most of all, he wished Emma were here. He thought she and Kacey would really hit it off and that Liam would approve.

While they were visiting over ice cream later, Amelia stared up at him and when he tossed the little girl an awkward smile, she returned it along with a question. "Is your girlfriend going to be here soon?"

"Amelia..." Kacey offered an apologetic smile. "We were...speculating on the way here that there probably was a girlfriend. Not that it's any of our business, *Amelia*."

"Mom said you'd have a girlfriend 'cause you're good-lookin'."

"Amelia Jane! Would you cut it out."

Tadhg laughed, feeling flattered. "Well, sorry to disappoint. There's no girlfriend. Well, there's sort of one. We're still figuring things out," he told Kacey, then turned to his niece. "Maybe you'll meet her next time, squirt."

He immediately wished he hadn't said anything because he had a feeling this little girl wouldn't forget. And if things ended up fizzling with Emma, he really didn't want to be reminded a year from now, or whenever he next saw Liam's family.

"Leave poor Uncle Tadhg alone, Amelia." Liam turned to him. "Is there someplace we could go for a run? Get away from these little monsters? I need to get my shoes out of the car, but I can drive."

"Sure. But we can just run from here. It's about a two-minute walk to the track."

"Great." He turned to his wife. "You okay with that, babe?"

"Sure," she said. "I'll beat these two in a game of Slap Jack while you're gone."

"No way!" Ethan dove for a deck of cards. "I'll beat you."

"I'll meet you down at the car." Laughing, Tadhg went to change his clothes.

The brothers hadn't run a quarter of a mile before Liam slowed his pace and grilled him about the girlfriend. "Is this somebody you're serious about? Do we get to meet her?"

Tadhg shrugged, then gave his brother a slightly more detailed account than he'd given Izzy last weekend. "It just seems like right now isn't a great time to spill everything about my 'checkered past'." He chalked quote marks in the air as they ran. "It wouldn't be right to let things go any further until she knows, but I can't pile that on her when she's already feeling so betrayed."

His brother shook his head. "I see what you mean. Man, that's wild that she found out from a DNA test. I thought the days of adoption being a big secret were over."

"That's what Emma said. But I think maybe there's something a little...deeper to this one."

"Oh? Like?"

He frowned. "I really have no idea. I haven't met her mom yet, but why would she feel obligated to keep a secret even after the birth mother is dead and gone?"

"That is strange. Well, I hope it all works out. For her, but for you and her, too." He lowered his head. "If she's half as great a woman as Kacey, grab her. No matter what."

"Yeah, Kacey seems great. I mean, I don't know her that well, but if she's put up with you this long she must be quite a woman."

He got a hard punch in the tiger bicep for that. It hurt, but he'd never felt closer to his brother and that was worth any level of pain.

EMMA OPENED the fridge in the breezeway and inspected the flowers she'd picked up from the florist. They still looked fresh and it had finally cooled down enough outside that she could go harvest what she needed for the other wedding bouquets.

Once a wedding was over and everything had gone off without a hitch, she loved this part of her job. But when the flowers were still in the garden and anything from weather to bugs to a herd of deer or a family of raccoons could sabotage her efforts, she wasn't sure it was worth the stress.

She checked the bride's notes, put on some headphones and some good jazz, and headed for the garden with Bud trailing behind her. It didn't take long to fill her trug basket with a great selection of flowers for the table vases. She took those inside and put them in water before going back to choose blooms for the bouquets and boutonnières.

Once inside, she switched from jazz to a podcast, which had proven to crowd out the troubling thoughts more effectively. By the time she went to bed at ten, the flower fridge on the back porch—a regular refrigerator that she'd rigged with a circulating fan and extra humidity—was full of boxes of carefully labeled bouquets and vases. Now, if she could get them to the church tomorrow without ruining anything, she could relax.

She chose a comfy but frilly dress from her closet and set out shoes to match. Her job tomorrow was to install some hurricanes on the front pews, help the wedding party with their flowers, and get vases on the tables at the reception venue. She rarely stayed for the whole wedding, but she was often still there when guests started to arrive, so she'd learned to dress to fit in.

She finished listening to a podcast while she got ready for bed, but as soon as it ended and silence filled her bedroom, troubling thoughts bombarded her once again.

Suddenly, she dreaded going to a wedding tomorrow. In the past, weddings had been a chance to dream about her own special day, to think about how happy Mom would be to see her find that special someone, and to begin a precious new chapter of her life. But now, seeing happy families, a loving couple, and all the joy such days brought would only emphasize how completely alone in the world she was.

Chapter Nineteen

June

Emma parked her Malibu under the church's covered parking, pulling up as far as she could so she wouldn't be in anyone's way while she unloaded. She pulled down the visor and checked her reflection. No amount of makeup could disguise how little sleep she'd gotten last night, but at least the overcast sky offered soft light that was more forgiving. The forecast said rain was expected about the time guests would be arriving, and her heart went out to Marissa, the bride, who had no control over what the weather would do on this most special day of her life.

She texted the wedding coordinator to let her know she'd arrived and went around to open the trunk. One by one, she carried the boxes of bouquets and boutonnières into the foyer, leaving the box of vases for the reception tables in the car. Thankfully, it wasn't so hot that they would suffer for the short time they'd sit in the vehicle.

She lifted the lightest box and went in search of someone who could show her around. She'd done the flowers for a wedding at this church last summer, but the building had been remodeled since then, and she wasn't sure if the bride's room was still in the same place.

Halfway down a long hallway, an older woman approached her. "You must be the flower lady."

"Yes. Emma Fiori." She balanced the box on one arm and stretched out a hand to the woman. "Can you tell me where the bridal parties are dressing?"

"Follow me. Things are a little chaotic right now."

"Uh-oh. Is everything okay?"

The woman sighed. "It will be. I think."

A few minutes later, the woman opened a door on a bride in tears and her mother and three bridesmaids all trying to console her at once.

Emma tried to keep to the edge of the room, sorting flowers and waiting for an opening to talk with someone. She quickly deduced that the forecasted rain was the cause of Marissa's meltdown since she'd had her heart set on outdoor photos.

"The one day I needed to be perfect," the bride wailed. "It's ruined!"

Emma had to admit she was grateful it was the weather causing the bride's distress and not the flowers. Before every wedding, she had nightmares about ruining someone's special day because she didn't get the flowers right, or she was a boutonnière short or any other number of ways she could totally mess up a bride's wedding day.

Now, almost without thinking, she approached the little knot of women. "Oh, no, your day won't be ruined. In fact, I just checked the forecast a few minutes ago and by the time you head to the reception, the rain should let up."

The bride stared at her. "Are you sure?"

"I'm positive. No sunshine, but the rain is supposed to stop in less than an hour." She tapped her weather app and turned her phone toward Marissa. "And besides, this is the absolute best weather for getting great photos. The soft, overcast light makes everybody glow. You're going to have stunning wedding photos."

Marissa looked skeptical, but then her gaze moved past Emma to the boxes of flowers on the table where she'd staged them. "Oh, the flowers are here. They look gorgeous!"

The bridesmaids took the cue to lead Marissa over to the table. Emma disentangled the bridal bouquet from the rest and presented it to her, making sure the flowering jasmine trailed like it was supposed to.

"It's absolutely perfect," the bride's mother cooed, tossing Emma a look of profound gratitude.

"It did turn out really nice, didn't it. I love the colors you guys chose. If everything else looks okay to you, I'll take the grooms-men's flowers to them." She grabbed a disposable towel from the box that held the other bouquets. "They're all in water to keep them fresh till the last minute, so you'll want to wipe off the stems once you take them out of the vases so the water doesn't drip on your dresses."

"They're perfect." Marissa had regained her composure and mouthed a warm *thank-you*.

"I'll be back in a minute to see if anyone has a problem with their bouquets." Feeling relieved, Emma headed down the hall.

With twenty-five minutes till wedding time, all was calm in both bride's and groom's rooms and Emma headed back through the foyer to get the vases for the reception, which was being held in the church's gym.

A few guests loitered in the foyer and she slipped past them to the parking lot, thinking she'd drive around to the back of the church, but when she asked an usher standing outside where she should park, he informed her there wasn't a covered opening at the back. She decided to quickly bring them through the main door before the foyer was too crowded with guests.

True to the forecast, it was pouring rain outside and she could see a few people sitting in their cars, presumably waiting out the storm. There were four boxes, which meant four trips, but she didn't want to risk dumping a box of glass vases so she carried the first one inside and down the hall to the gym.

The church's gymnasium had been transformed thanks to massive swoops of fabric dotted with fairy lights that effectively lowered the ceiling and hid basketball hoops and other athletic paraphernalia. A group of women bustled about putting table-cloths on round tables. A lot of tables. The bride had ordered arrangements for twenty tables, but Emma did a quick count and came up with twenty-five. Great. Now what?

She approached an older woman who looked like she was in charge and introduced herself. "They only ordered twenty vases. Do you know what they want for the other five tables?"

"Oh. I didn't think about that. They were trying to cram ten people at each of these tables and we decided that was too many, so we made an executive decision and added five tables for eight people at each." She waved another woman over and explained the situation.

The woman shrugged. "I guess we'll just have five tables without decorations."

Emma frowned. "Is anything else going on the tables besides these flower arrangements?"

"There's some sparkly confetti stuff, but we can make that stretch."

"Okay. And I bet there are some vases in the kitchen. Or even just drinking glasses that would work," Emma said. "Let me bring in the rest of the flowers and I can split them up and get five more arrangements. We don't want anyone to feel left out." She wished people wouldn't make "executive decisions" that contradicted the bride's plans. At least there didn't seem to be a seating chart or place cards for the tables, so it wouldn't completely destroy planned seating.

She found some small juice glasses in the kitchen that would serve well and filled them with water, placing them by the first box of vases. If the clock in the kitchen was right, she still had plenty of time before the guests would start arriving for the reception. She headed back for another load of vases.

Cars were bumper to bumper under the overhang now with

heroic drivers dropping off their guests while they went to park in a deluge. As she lifted another box from the trunk of her car, a man ran across the parking lot, but stopped by her car when he spotted her. He glanced pointedly at the boxes of vases remaining in the trunk. "Can I help you with those?"

She hesitated, judging by his suit and tie that this was a wedding guest. "Oh, you don't need to do that. But thank you."

"No problem. If you can put those in my arms, I think I can safely carry two of them."

"Are you sure?"

"Of course. Here—" He reached for the box she'd just lifted out and secured it between his waist and a muscled arm. She put a second box in his hands and lifted the other one, balancing it in one arm while she closed the trunk. "Thank you so much."

"No problem. Just show me where they go."

An usher held the door for them and the man followed Emma inside. "Hang on just a minute, okay?"

She watched as he went toward a woman who stood waiting with two young children, a boy and a younger girl.

"Wait here," he told them. "I'm going to carry these boxes down to the reception for her."

"Sure." The woman offered Emma a smile, then turned to the little girl and straightened the bow in her hair.

She walked briskly toward the gym, aware of the stranger following her, praying he wouldn't drop a box, yet immensely grateful for his help since she hadn't counted on having to completely redo the vases. "Thank you so much for doing this."

"You're most welcome."

His voice seemed strangely familiar and she wondered if she'd met him somewhere before.

"This might be a strange question, but"—he gave her a little smile—"is your name, by chance, Emma?"

She stopped in the middle of the hallway and turned to face him. "It is. Have we met?"

He laughed. "No, but I think you know my little brother. Tadhg McKay? I'm Liam. Tadhg's brother."

"No wonder your voice sounded familiar to me. But... How did you know who I am?"

"It's crazy. We're here from Ohio—for the wedding, obviously. My wife and Marissa are college friends. But Tadhg just happened to mention that he knew you... He was telling us about your farm and he mentioned you were doing the flowers for a wedding this weekend. I'm sure there's probably a wedding in every church on the island today, but I just finally put things together—flowers, wedding, pretty girl..." He looked embarrassed by that last comment.

"Yeah, that's kind of crazy that your wedding was the same as mine. What are the chances, huh? Well, its nice to meet you. Tadhg has talked about you and...is it Declan?"

"That's right. I'd hate to guess what he's told you about his crazy brothers." His grin looked so much like Tadhg's when he teased her.

"Oh, nothing too bad." She laughed as if she was joking, but it was an honest answer. To avoid further questions from him, she turned and hurried on to the kitchen.

She showed him where to set the flowers and thanked him again.

"No problem. I'll have to tell Tadhg I met you. Glad I finally figured it out."

She laughed, feeling awkward—and wondering what Tadhg had told him about her. "Yes. Tell him hi...from me."

"Of course, will do." He started to leave, then turned back to her. "Good luck with the wedding. Your flowers look great. They smell good too." He shrugged and feigned a sniff at the crook of his elbow where the flowers had rested. "I couldn't help but notice."

Her smile turned genuine. "It's probably the Confederate jasmine you're smelling. It's my favorite fragrance. And thanks again for your help."

She watched him walk away, suddenly seeing Tadhg clearly in the gait of his older brother. She wished she could have met Tadhg's sister-in-law and niece and nephew. If she'd known who they were, she would have introduced herself. But she had work to do now. And time was getting away from her.

But as she reworked the vases, pulling three or four blooms from each to create new arrangements for the extra tables, Liam's words—which were actually Tadhg's words—kept playing in her mind. *Flowers, wedding, pretty girl.* And she couldn't help but smile and feel a tiny spark of hope. If Tadhg had told his brother about her, especially in those terms, maybe everything wasn't as over as she'd thought it was.

Chapter Twenty

Tadhg flipped the page in the novel he was reading, C.S. Lewis's *Till We Have Faces*—an effort sparked by Emma's chiding him for only reading non-fiction. But after several pages, he realized he hadn't retained anything he'd read. It wasn't even ten p.m. but he was already in bed for the night.

He and Liam's family had rented bikes and ridden the trails at Jekyll Island this morning—something he didn't remember from family vacations, but Liam did. The live oaks along the winding trails were in their full glory, layered with lush resurrection ferns and dripping with Spanish moss. He thought those oaks, more than anything else, gave the island its mystery and appeal.

It had been a fun, but tiring day with Liam, Kacey, and the kids, and since they were busy with a friend's wedding this evening and had plans to take the kids to some museums on Sunday afternoon, he wouldn't see them again until Monday when they met for an early lunch in Pier Village before starting the drive back to Ohio.

He'd have to keep their lunch short since he'd already taken the afternoon off from work on Friday. They were swamped and still short-handed with Brian out sick. Jillian hadn't been too happy about him taking off early.

He started another chapter but found it hard to concentrate and finally turned off the lamp. Almost immediately, his phone buzzed on the dresser. He switched the light back on and checked his texts, surprised to find a message from Emma.

Emma: You'll never guess who I ran into tonight.

Tadhg: I give up. Who?

Emma: Somebody from Ohio.

Tadhg: Somebody I know?

He liked that she was texting him as if nothing had ever gone south between them, but at the same time, it made him wonder what she was up to.

Emma: Somebody you know well.

Tadhg: My brother's the only one I can think of from Ohio. He's here for a wedding this weekend. Wait! Was that YOUR wedding?

He hit Send, then realizing how that might sound, instantly sent a correction.

Tadhg: Not YOUR wedding, obviously, but the one you did flowers for?

Emma: Yes! Liam helped me carry boxes into the church in the rain. He reminds me so much of YOU!

Tadhg: Except much older, right??

An LOL emoji appeared and he smiled, waiting for her to say more. Hoping she would.

> Emma: Are you having a good visit with your brother? Did you know they were coming?

> Tadhg: Liam called last Sunday night. Right after we talked.

Right after you broke up with me, he thought. But didn't say. Before she read something snarky into that, he texted again:

> Tadhg: You'd be proud of me... I made supper for them last night at my apartment.

> Emma: Wow. What did you make? Bologna sandwiches?

> Tadhg: Ha! I'll have you know I made a pot roast with potatoes and carrots, a berry salad, and ice cream for dessert. (Well, I didn't make the ice cream—or the berries—but still...give me some credit!)

> Emma: Haha! I'm impressed. (Pretty sure God made the roast, potatoes, and carrots too. Just sayin'.)

Another happy face. And the whole conversation was making him feel pretty happy.

> Tadhg: Wow, you sure know how to bring a man down...

He deleted the comment before hitting Send. He didn't want to risk hurting her feelings. But he scrambled to think of something else to say. He didn't want the conversation to end.

> Tadhg: I concede. God wins. Then I guess I can rave about how delicious it all was, right?

> Emma: Rave away! ☺

While he composed a lame text—anything to keep her talking—she texted again:

> Emma: Hey, I know it's late, but could I call you? I'll make it quick.

> Tadhg: Absolutely.

His phone rang and he quickly clicked Accept. "Hi. That's pretty cool you met my brother."

"I know." He heard a smile in her voice. "He seems really nice. I didn't get to meet his family, but I saw them in the lobby."

"It's been good having them here." He told her about riding bikes on Jekyll this morning. "We should do that sometime. Apparently my family did that every year until I came along. At least I don't remember ever doing that with them. My memories are more of the beach and the pool at the hotel."

"How long are they here for?"

"Oh, they head back tomorrow. We're having lunch together first."

"That's nice. Well, I don't want to keep you too late but... I feel like I owe you an apology."

"An apology?" It was a parry. He knew what she owed him an apology for, but it didn't seem like he should acknowledge that.

"Tadhg, I know I've been a huge grouch ever since—well, ever since you've met me basically."

He laughed. "I think that might be hyperbole."

"Well, at least since this whole mess with the stupid DNA test. You probably don't even believe I *can* be a nice person."

"No, I understand. It was a tough thing to find out."

"It is, but that doesn't make it right for me to take it out on you."

"I don't blame you, Emma. And with an exception or two, I think you've taken it pretty well."

"Well, you don't know everything."

"Uh-oh. Did you find out something...else?"

"No, but I...I did a terrible thing. And I got caught."

"Caught?"

"It's a lot to explain over the phone. If you aren't too mad at me, would you be willing to get together...again? And I'll explain everything."

"I'd like that a lot."

"I'm warning you though... You might think I'm a horrible person after I tell you what I did."

He took the opening without thinking, but it seemed too perfect to let it slide. "I'll tell you what: I have some things I need to tell you too. And then you might think *I'm* a horrible person. Maybe we can have a contest to see who's the horrible-est."

She laughed. "I'm not sure that's something to aspire to. But maybe we can be horrible people together?"

"It's probably no contest, but hey, bring your best game."

"Game on." He could tell she was smiling. "But seriously, I'd like to get this over with. When were you thinking?"

"Does tomorrow night work? It might have to be kind of late. We have a guy out sick at work and they're killing us with overtime."

"That's okay. I don't have anything else on. How about I make supper."

"Bologna sandwiches?"

"Ha! I'll try to do better than that."

"I'd be happy to eat bologna with you. But hey, I have tons of leftovers from Friday night's dinner."

"The dinner God made?"

"That's the one. Why don't you come here?"

"That'd be nice."

"I'll call you when I leave work, but I'll try to get out of there as close to six as I can. That okay?"

"Sure. Just call me. Oh, and send me your address."

He hung up and shook his head. He was on a roller coaster for sure. And frankly, he'd never been a fan of roller coasters.

EMMA SLOWED the Malibu and peered through the windshield looking for the address Tadhg had texted her. She pulled around behind an older two-story house with a sweet cottage garden in the front. She was glad she'd thought to bring flowers for Izzy, Tadhg's adopted grandma.

The memory of those conversations made her smile. But she sobered, remembering why she was here. Tadhg might not think very highly of her after she told him how she'd violated Mom's and Bill's privacy. Her mother was probably the one she should be talking to tonight, but Mom had made it clear she needed a "break" from Emma. And who could blame her?

With a sigh, dreading the conversation to come, she grabbed the vase of flowers from the cupholder, closed the car door, and started up the steep stairs to Tadhg's apartment, holding tight to the railing.

He opened the door before she reached the landing at the top. "Hey there. Can I take those for you?"

She handed the flowers up to him. "They're for...Izzy." She'd almost said, "for your grandma," but despite the fact she believed him when he said he'd been joking, it was still kind of a sore spot for her. Especially now that she was on the other side of the lies and deceit. She wished they could talk before they ate dinner. Her stomach was a kaleidoscope of butterflies. But it might be much worse *after* they talked.

Tadhg answered the question for her when she stepped inside. "I'm sorry, but a breaker blew and the stupid crockpot didn't come on. I'm having to heat things up in the oven the old-fashioned way, so it'll be a little while, but I've got some chips and salsa we can eat while we wait."

"It smells good." She waited for her eyes to adjust and looked around the apartment, surprised to find an eclectic collection of vintage leather furniture and throw pillows in masculine fabrics. The effect was cozy and intentional. "I really like your place. And look at you, keeping all these plants alive." For a minute, she wondered if the place had come furnished and Izzy got credit for the decor.

As if he'd read her mind, he said, "Izzy gave me the plants the first winter I lived here, but I've kept them alive all by my lonesome—well, with a couple of exceptions, God rest their souls. But don't be too impressed. It's just a bunch of thrifted and Facebook Marketplace stuff that I thought looked good together."

She winced. "I hate to admit it, but that painting would have looked awfully nice in here."

He laughed. "I think it's in the right place. Have a seat and I'll get us something to drink."

She took a seat on a leather sofa in a bay window alcove where she had a view of the entire apartment.

Tadhg stepped into the sunny, open kitchen and got a jar of salsa from the fridge. He poured some into two small, mismatched bowls and brought them, along with a fresh bag of chips, to the coffee table. "Iced tea or Coke?"

"Whatever you're having. I like both."

When he returned with large tumblers of iced tea and a roll of paper towels, he settled into an overstuffed chair beside the sofa, then opened the bag of chips. He tore off sections of paper toweling and gave them each two. He put a handful of chips on one square and another paper towel on his lap for a napkin. "Sorry, I'm not fancy here."

"No, it's perfect." She did the same, then dipped a chip and ate it.

He came right to the point. "So, what's this awful thing you did? Might as well get it off your chest so you can enjoy supper when it's ready."

"You don't want to go first?"

"Not unless you want me to."

"No, I'm pretty sure mine's worse. I'll go first." She hesitated, then blew out a sigh. "You're going to think I'm terrible, but I went to my mom's last Sunday...while they were out of town. I searched through her desk trying to find my adoption papers—or *something* that would tell me who my parents are—who *I* am."

"Did you find anything?" Tadhg took a sip of tea and waited.

"Nothing. And my mom was furious. She's not speaking to me." She told him more about what had happened. "I can't blame her really, but my mom was my best friend, she was like the sister I never had and now—" She couldn't say more, and to her own surprise, she burst into tears.

"I'm so sorry, Emma." He shook his head, obviously at a loss for words.

"This whole thing is just making me crazy. I never would have done something like that before—going into their house without permission. For the record, I had keys to their house, but I had no right to go through her things. I think the thing that made Mom the maddest is that it's Bill's house too. And he doesn't have anything to do with this."

"Do you think he knows...the story of your birth?"

"He'd better not. If some man who's not even related to any of us knows and I don't..." She felt the anger surging back.

"I understand why you feel that way, but would you keep a secret like that from your husband?"

She knew well the weight of his question, but she deflected. "I wouldn't keep a secret like this from my *daughter*."

Tadhg was quiet for a long minute. "Emma, can I say something about this?" He held up a hand. "It's none of my business and if you'd rather I just stay out of it, please say so. I'd understand."

"No. Go ahead." But she didn't think she was going to like what he had to say.

Chapter Twenty-One

Tadhg sucked in a breath and exhaled slowly. He'd thought a lot about her situation, and while he empathized with her, he had to admit that he didn't think he would be quite so distraught if the same had happened to him. But yesterday in church, he'd gotten a little different perspective on things and he'd been praying about whether he should share it with her. This seemed the opening he'd been looking for.

"I want to say this carefully, but the thing I keep coming back to is that you are exactly the same person you were before you took"—he chalked quotation marks in the air—"'that stupid test.' That test didn't change anything about who you are, Emma. You are still the product of both your birth parents and your adoptive parents and they both gave you good things. Your birth parents made a gorgeous woman...physically. And sorry, I can't help but notice. I'm talking *gorgeous*."

She smiled at the compliment, but her expression quickly turned wary. "Go on."

"And your adoptive parents made you the warm, funny, sweet, talented woman you are. And they passed down their faith in God. Maybe you wouldn't have had that chance with your birth parents. I don't know, but... Hang on a sec." He rose and went into the bedroom and returned with a Bible. "I'm going to go Bible-thumper on you for a minute, okay?"

She merely shrugged.

He turned to the first chapter of Ephesians and skimming quickly to the part he felt applied to her situation, read, "...Blessed be the God and Father of our Lord Jesus Christ, who has blessed us in Christ with every spiritual blessing in the heavenly places, even as he *chose* us..." He emphasized the word and continued. "...in him before the foundation of the world, that we should be holy and blameless before him. In love he predestined us for *adoption* to himself as sons through Jesus Christ, according to the purpose of his will." He looked up to see whether he'd lost her.

But she was listening intently.

"First of all, Emma, God obviously values adoption greatly. In a sense, when we belong to Him, we're all adopted. And God uses that to accomplish His will. I know it might be stretching it a tiny bit to apply this to human adoption, but I do think the general idea of God's opinion of adoption applies. Can I read a little bit more?"

She nodded, waiting.

He ran his finger down the pages, looking for the verses Pastor Shelton had quoted. There it was, verse 11. "In him we have obtained an *inheritance*—" Again, he emphasized the word. "... having been predestined according to the purpose of him who works all things according to the counsel of his will..."

He stopped, holding his finger on the next verse. "It's kind of like Romans 8:28, the whole idea that when we belong to God, everything works together for good—even the hard stuff. I don't know if that helps at all, but I just hope you know that even though it might feel like it, you really don't need to 'find yourself' or figure out who you are now. You're the very same person, Emma. The same wonderful person I met."

She dipped her head. "It doesn't feel like it."

"I understand you wanting to have answers. I get that. And I definitely understand you feeling betrayed because your parents lied to you about your adoption—or at least kept it from you."

"Mom says she never lied. And I have to be honest, looking back, I can't think of anything she ever told me that wasn't true—at least not that I know of. But lying doesn't always involve *telling* a lie. Sometimes it's what you *don't* say that's the lie."

He felt like she'd punched him in the gut. "Okay, ouch."

She shot him a questioning look.

"That hit pretty close to home. I don't mean to change the subject, but that's what I needed to...*confess* to you. I haven't exactly lied to you, but there are some things I've avoided telling you because they're hard. And I'm afraid they'll be deal-breakers for you."

"Like?"

He reached over and briefly touched her knee. "I really didn't mean to turn the subject on me."

"It's okay. We can take turns." She gave a weak smile.

"Okay." He leaned forward, meeting her gaze. "I made it a point to tell you that when I was in my wild days, I hadn't gone to prison. That's true. But I *did* go to jail." He watched her face but her expression was enigmatic. "It was a wakeup call, and for that, I'm grateful. But I have a record, Emma. A *criminal* record." He made himself use the word. "They were misdemeanor charges, not felonies, but because of that record, I'd likely never get a teaching job. That's why I haven't gone back to school to finish my degree. What good would it do?"

"How long were you in jail?" Her voice sounded detached. "And...why?"

"The charges were assault, disorderly conduct, and disorderly intoxication. A bar fight. Not my first, and the judge had seen me in his courtroom one too many times. He sentenced me to two weeks in jail minus the two days I'd already served." There. He'd told her. Now it was up to God.

Emma said nothing, and her silence scared him, but he stayed silent himself. He'd known this would take some time for her to process. To decide whether it was something she could forgive or not.

When her silence went on for an overlong minute, he said, "I'll answer any questions you have. And...if you decide it's something you can't live with, I understand. I...I promise I didn't intend to keep this from you for so long, but after what happened with your DNA test, it didn't seem right to lay that on you too."

She gave a nod. "I understand. And you haven't had any other...*issues* since that time? You're not...an alcoholic or—"

"No. Nothing like that. I haven't had—or even wanted—a drink since I moved here. But..." He ran a hand through his hair. "As long as we're laying it all on the line, you should also know that I still owe about eight thousand dollars on school loans—for a degree I never got and a job I'll never have. That really rankles me. But it *was* over twenty thousand dollars not that long ago, and I'm doing everything I can to get the rest paid off completely as soon as I possibly can."

She shook her head. "That part doesn't bother me, Tadhg. Almost everybody our age has school loans."

"Yes, but most people are making good money on whatever their degree was for."

"It seems like your job pays okay...right?"

"It pays the bills and the overtime has helped pay down my loans. But if it wasn't for Izzy's low rent and what extra I make on the furniture and stuff, I'd be struggling. No," he corrected himself, "I just wouldn't be living *on* the island. I'd be in Brunswick or somewhere cheaper close by."

"I'm in the same boat, Tadhg. If I hadn't inherited my house and land, there's no way I could live on the island on just what the flowers and weddings bring in. I have to be really careful with money. But I'm living my dream. And...living on Saint Simons was your dream, right?"

He lifted one shoulder in a shrug, dismissing her comment.

"I've had a lot of dreams. Most of them haven't come true. But that's the consequence for living the way I did. I recognize that."

"I'm not sure that's how things work, but even if it was, that doesn't mean you have to quit dreaming."

"I guess I never thought about it that way. I'm not unhappy, Emma."

"I know, but you still should dream. Work toward the life you want. Are you sure you couldn't get a teaching job, Tadhg? Surely there are places that would hire you despite your...record."

"Right now, I'm pretty grateful that Cable Solutions was willing to take me on. If I'd served time for theft or breaking and entering, I wouldn't even have been able to get a job as a cable tech." He frowned. "People tend to not like letting criminals into their homes."

"Oh." She matched his frown. "I never thought about that."

"And there's still that degree I don't have. And those loans that need paid off. I sure don't want to take out more." He cocked his head, challenging her to find a way around that one.

"It doesn't all have to happen overnight. You're still young." An ornery spark lit her eyes. "Well, relatively young." Her eyes looked more green than hazel today, probably because of the emerald green shirt she wore.

"Speaking of which, don't you have a birthday this month—Emma June?"

She nodded, looking pleased that he'd remembered. "The twenty-fifth." But as soon as she said that, she bit her bottom lip. "I'm not sure I'll even celebrate it this year. I've always celebrated with my mom." Her eyes filled with a glitter of tears that threatened to spill over.

He slid to the sofa beside her, daring to put an arm around her shoulders, telling himself he could not let the moment turn romantic no matter how much he wanted it to. "I'm sorry. I hope things will be mended between you by then."

"I don't see how they can be."

"Can I say something, Emma?" He scooted away, pressing his back against the arm of the sofa, angling his body toward her.

"Okay?" She said it as a question.

"I just don't want you to let this ruin your life—like I almost did. I realize I didn't know you very long before this happened, but it seemed like you were always so cheerful before—happy with your life, happy in your work, confident in who you are. Just...please take it to heart that nothing has changed. God has always known exactly who you are, who He made you to be and not one thing changed between the moment before you opened those stupid test results and the moment after. Do you believe that?"

Her whole body sighed. "I want to believe it. I do, Tadhg, but how can I? I was lied to. That changes everything."

"I understand how it changes your trust. In other people. Maybe even in God. I hope not." He looked at her, wishing for some indication if that was true. "But we're all imperfect people. I'm so sorry for the ways that I was deceitful to you. It was self-protection. That doesn't make it right, but hopefully understand-able. I'm sure it's the same for your mom. And in my case, Emma, it was because I liked you so much, I didn't want to risk losing the chance at a...friendship with you. Isn't it possible that your mom's reasons are similar. I don't know what her reasons are, but maybe it's something she's afraid would keep her from a relationship with you."

She gave a wry laugh. "Ironic, isn't it? Because that's exactly what's happened. No, she keeps saying that she made a promise she can't break."

"Then honor that, Emma. I know it's hard, but trust your mom to be doing the right thing, even though it seems wrong and impossible for you. Maybe she'll come around. But there's really nothing you can do to force it out of her."

She shook her head, eyes down. "No. God knows I've tried."

"I'm sorry. I probably overstepped my privilege there. I just hate seeing you so crushed by this. And even more than that, I hate that it's created a rift in your relationship with your mom."

"I hate it too."

"Spending time with Liam and his family made me regret the way I've pulled away from my family. But that's on me. You can't control what your mom decides, but at least don't let it be on you."

"You're blessed to have a big family." She took a shuddering breath and suddenly began to weep in a way that frightened him.

He moved closer and put an arm around her again.

"I'm sorry," she said after the sobs subsided. "I just feel so... *alone.*"

He wanted to tell her that God was always with her. And that she had Tadhg McKay's heart. But she already knew the former, and it was too soon for the latter. And for all he knew, the latter might feel like a burden to her right now. So he kept silent.

Chapter Twenty-Two

Emma yanked weeds from the raised beds and stuffed a bushel basket full, then deadheaded the zinnias and the dahlias, adding to the basket. She'd thought constantly about everything Tadhg had said yesterday. Her rational mind knew what he told her was true. Whether Mom was right or wrong in keeping such a heavy secret from her, it shouldn't change who she was, who Emma Fiori was. And she was doing her best to believe that her adoption into God's family was the only thing that mattered for eternity. She'd read the verses Tadhg showed her over and over again, and she was trying—as the fourth chapter of Ephesians said—*to be made new in the attitude of her mind and to put on the new self, created to be like God in true right-eousness and holiness.*

Still, it was a constant struggle. It was too tempting to jump down to the very next verse about putting away falsehood and speaking the truth in love, and to use those words like a dagger toward her mom. Like the dog in the Bible that kept coming back to its vomit, she kept coming back to the hurt and pain and betrayal.

But she was determined to return instead to the verses that

told her to let all bitterness and wrath and anger be put away. "Be kind to one another, tenderhearted, forgiving one another, as God in Christ forgave you," the verses said. God had forgiven her of so much, and she knew she needed to forgive Mom, whether she ever came around or not. But that was so much easier said than done.

Tadhg had walked her down the steep fire-escape stairway of his apartment last night and wrapped her in a hug beside her car before opening the door for her. She thought it was only a hug meant to comfort. And it had. But it also made her long for something more with him, and it had taken everything she had not to turn his embrace into that something more.

But she recognized how vulnerable she was. And she was grateful when Tadhg invited her to go out with him next weekend but suggested they meet at the pier for a walk and dinner at a restaurant. Maybe he was feeling vulnerable too?

She was coming in from the garden with the basket of weeds when her phone trilled with a text in the back pocket of her overall shorts. The sound made her heart jump every time, hoping it was Mom. It had been a full week now since Mom had told her they needed to "take a break"—whatever that meant. She'd tried calling once a couple days after Mom and Bill had been at her house, but Mom hadn't answered her phone, and Emma had been afraid to try again because the thought of her mom rejecting her again broke her heart.

She dusted her hands off on the bib of her overalls and slipped her phone from her pocket. It wasn't Mom, but seeing Tadhg's crinkle-eyed smile in his photo she'd put on her phone made her smile back. She slipped off her Crocs and went inside, hurriedly washed her hands, then opened her messages.

Tadhg: Am I bothering you?

Emma: Not at all. I just came in from the garden. Did you get off early?

Tadhg: No, I'm on my way to my last appointment. Can't talk long, but I just wanted to see how you're doing.

She thought for a minute before answering, wanting to be honest with him.

Emma: I'm okay. Still sad I haven't heard from Mom, but it made me smile to see your name on my phone.

Tadhg: Good. Glad I texted then. We're still on for Friday night, right?

Emma: I'm counting on it. I'll get stuff ready for the farmers market Friday afternoon so I don't have to worry about getting up too early.

Tadhg: You're sure that doesn't throw your schedule off? We could do Saturday night if that works better.

Emma: Don't you dare cancel on me. I'm looking forward to it.

He sent a smiley face and a pink heart and that was the end of his messages for the evening. And she liked that.

There were so many things she liked about him. If she and her mom were on speaking terms, she was pretty sure she wouldn't tell her—at least not yet—about what Tadhg had revealed about his past. She still had trouble picturing him in a bar fight. Drunk. Getting arrested. She rubbed her eyes, not liking the images that appeared in her mind's eye. But she believed what Tadhg had said about it all being in the past. She trusted him.

She'd never gone through a full-on rebellion as a teenager, but she'd done plenty of foolish things, and she wouldn't have wanted

Tadhg to judge her on the immature girl she'd been six or seven years ago. For the first time, she wondered how she would have reacted if Mom had told her about the adoption when she was a teenager. Would it have caused her to rebel? Was that part of why they hadn't told her? Because she hadn't exactly handled it like a mature adult when she found out at the ripe old age of almost twenty-eight.

Still, there was that promise her mom had made. It hounded her no matter how she tried to put it aside. There had to be something behind that promise—something that Mom felt should be kept secret from Emma about her own birth mother.

She pushed the thought aside and went to take a shower. Maybe she could wash away the nagging questions that may never have answers.

THE PIER TEEMED with noisy tourists and the usual Friday night locals fishing, picnicking, or just loitering on the pier. A jazz band played over in the park by the lighthouse and Tadhg was sorry he'd recommended such a chaotic place for their date. But he also knew he needed the protection a public place offered his heart against his growing desire for this woman walking beside him.

If Emma was aware of how he felt about her, she didn't let on. But he was determined to take it slower with her than he'd ever taken things before with any other woman. He wanted to be sure. Sure about her—which he was, but mostly sure that this was truly God's doing and not his own. But more importantly, he needed to guard Emma's heart. She seemed much more at peace tonight than she'd been at his house on Monday, but she still hadn't heard from her mom, and he knew that was as painful for her as the betrayal she felt or the uncertainty about the circumstances of her birth.

His goal tonight was simply to be a friend, a listening ear, and to help take her mind off those heavy things. As Jillian always said at work, it was a tough job, but somebody had to do it. He curbed a smile at the thought.

"What's so funny?" She peered up at him as they navigated the crowded pier, looking amused—and beautiful with the sea breezes whipping her hair around her sun-kissed face.

He looked across the water back to the sea wall, avoiding her curious gaze. "I was thinking about something at work."

"Want to share?"

"It's kind of a long story..." He hesitated. They'd both committed to being open and frank with each other. That didn't mean every single thought had to come to light, but in the interest of transparency, he tried to explain. "I was just hoping that bringing you here tonight might help keep your mind off of things."

She frowned up at him. "What does that have to do with work?"

"Our office manager always says"—he affected a falsetto, imitating Jillian—"'It's a tough job, but somebody has to do it.' I was laughing because that's how I feel about tonight. The tough job of spending time with you, I mean. Don't take that wrong," he said quickly. "You know that saying is facetious, right?"

"Awww, that's sweet of you. But I don't want you to feel like you have to tiptoe around me, Tadhg. I'm doing okay. Really, I am. And it does help to get out and do things, so thank you for doing the tough job."

They leaned on the railing side by side, staring across to where the Saint Simons Lighthouse rose through the trees near the rocky shore. He had a sudden memory of a family vacation when they'd done a tour of the lighthouse and climbed the stairs to the top. "Have you ever been up in the lighthouse?"

"Not since I was little. But I remember loving it—even if it was a little scary. Have you?"

He nodded and told her about his memory. "I think one of

the things I liked so much about those vacations was that my brothers' friends weren't around, so they treated me like an equal. Not that they ever bullied me or anything. We just didn't have much in common back home because they were so much older."

"Liam doesn't look that much older...I don't think."

"It's strange. He did feel more like a peer when they were here. It was kind of cool."

"Maybe Declan and his family will come sometime too. And your parents."

"Speaking of which, you'll be happy to know I've called my mom twice already this month." Too late he realized it might feel to her like he was rubbing it in.

But if she noticed, she didn't react. "Good for you. See? I'm a good influence on you."

"Yes, you are." He pulled her into a side hug, but quickly let go. "Are you hungry yet? Maybe it won't be so crazy on the pier after dinner." They'd agreed on a restaurant a couple of blocks from the pier.

"I'm ready whenever you are. Maybe we can come back down here for the sunset. That's my favorite thing."

"Sure." He put a hand lightly at the small of her back and steered her around a gaggle of loud teenagers who were hanging out in the middle of the pier.

They talked all through dinner and were both surprised that it was almost dark when they stepped outside.

"Oh! We're going to miss the sunset," Emma said.

"We can still make it. Follow me. I know a shortcut." He took her hand and led her down Beachview Drive and across the lawn in front of the library. They climbed the steps and walked through the covered meeting room to the rear of the building, then back down onto the lawn that cut through to Neptune Park.

There were still plenty of people wandering along the sidewalk that followed the rocky sea wall, but the pier had cleared off considerably and the sunset was a stunner. The covered pier and a stand of palm trees on the shore were silhouetted on a canvas of pink and orange and gold, made all the more dramatic by navy blue clouds overhead and the dark sea below.

Acutely aware of Emma's warm hand still in his, Tadhg did his best to hold her hand lightly so she would feel free to let go if it made her uncomfortable. But he wasn't one bit sorry when instead, she tightened her grip and moved closer to him.

Chapter Twenty-Three

Emma inhaled the sweet scent one last time before closing the flower fridge, grateful she had her blooms cut and ready to assemble for the wedding she was doing tomorrow. Tadhg had gotten tickets from somebody at work for a community theater production over in Brunswick tonight and had invited her to go with him. She'd been nervous about getting the flowers done in time for the afternoon ceremony, but she felt better now with the cutting done. She could easily put bouquets together after she got home tonight.

Their time together these last few weeks had been so sweet, and more importantly, it had kept her mind off of how much she missed Mom and of how uncertain her future seemed.

She and Tadhg had texted almost daily since that night on the pier, and she loved his creativity in figuring out ways to spend time together. No mere dinner-and-a-movie with this guy. He preferred seven a.m. garage sale dates, walking on the pier, and community theater. They planned to get Thai food after the show, and it crossed her mind that it might be after midnight before they got home, but she would stay up as late as she needed to.

She had a few hours before he picked her up so she watered

her houseplants, tidied up the kitchen, and laid out her supplies on the dining room table ready to assemble flowers tonight. When she was finished with that, she plugged her phone in to charge and checked her messages one last time before heading for the shower. Every time she looked at her phone, she still hoped beyond hope that there would be a message or a voicemail from Mom. It had been almost four weeks now without so much as a text. A month! It killed her, yet she couldn't seem to find the courage to take the first step and risk another rejection. And if she did call Mom, was she willing to let it go, to tell her mother that she didn't need the answers she'd asked for? She wasn't sure. And until she was, it wouldn't be right to stir the hornets' nest again.

In the beginning, she'd fantasized about hiring a detective or an attorney, about going to the hospital where she'd been born and asking for her records—doing whatever it took to get the answers she so desperately longed for. But these last few weeks with Tadhg had tempered her anger and even her curiosity. She'd dived into the book of Ephesians, where so many of the verses Tadhg had shared with her came from. She'd found solace there. But whether she would admit it to him or not, she'd also prayed that before she turned twenty-eight, she might have closure on this whole ugly chapter. The clock was ticking fast on that. Her birthday was next Tuesday.

An hour later, fresh from the shower with hair and makeup done and ready for the theater in a long sundress, she was slipping on her shoes when her phone rang. She smiled. She'd set Tadhg's ring to "Eye of the Tiger"—mostly so she'd know it *wasn't* Mom —but Tadhg's song made her smile every time.

"Hey," he said in that sweet drawn-out voice meant only for her. "Just letting you know I'm going to be a few minutes late. I got stuck at work longer than I intended."

"No problem. Do you want me to meet you there?"

"No, no… I'm leaving my house now."

"Okay, if you're sure. I wouldn't mind."

"No, I'm sure. I'll be there in a few."

She hung up and went to fluff the sofa pillows and trim brown leaves from the houseplants—things she did when she was nervous. She'd gotten used to the butterflies that came with Tadhg McKay. And she was grateful they always went away the minute she was actually with him. When they were together she felt at ease and frankly, more herself than she'd ever felt with another human, with the exception of her parents, and maybe Nonno and Nonni. But when they were apart, the very thought of him brought butterflies. No other guy had done that to her— well, at least not since Robby Harbow in seventh grade.

She wandered aimlessly out to the back porch and almost tripped over Bud, who was sprawled in the doorway. "You are going to be the death of me, cat!" She opened the flower fridge, just to mentally take inventory and make sure she'd cut everything she needed for the wedding. An icy vapor cloud puffed from the door, and frigid air hit her face. That was odd. It wasn't so hot on the porch that there should be that kind of condensation. She stuck her hand in the fridge. It felt like a deep freeze. She pulled out a vase and a larger bucket of flowers that was covering up the temperature control dial.

"What in the world...?" It was set at the lowest temperature. She must have inadvertently moved the dial when she shoved that last vase in. The vase in her hands was freezing cold, and ice had begun to form around the edges of the water inside. Worse, the flowers were starting to freeze! They looked fine now, but once they thawed, they would turn into a mushy, wilted mess. Especially the roses, and those were the main attraction in this bride's bouquets. Even if she had time to cut everything again, she didn't think she had enough blooms in the garden to replace these.

She pulled the vases and buckets out one by one and set them on the counter beside the fridge. She wanted to cry. The ones on the upper shelves might be okay—at least there was no ice in those vases—but she wouldn't know for sure for a few hours until they thawed.

One thing was sure, she wasn't going anywhere tonight. She

had to see what she could salvage, cut and de-thorn more roses, and maybe go buy some grocery store flowers to fill in if things were as bad as she feared.

She heaved a sigh and kicked off her fancy shoes. Oh, and she'd better catch Tadhg before he came all the way here.

He answered on the first ring. "I am so sorry, Tadhg, but you're going to have to go without me."

"Why? What happened?"

She gave a little growl, all the more frustrated as she realized she was giving up a fun evening with him. "I have a major flower emergency." She explained what had happened, apologizing again.

"Is there anything I can do to help?"

"No, it'll be okay. I just have to wait an hour or two and see what survived and then go cut everything again to replace what-ever didn't make it."

"Let me come and help."

"No, I hate to make you miss the show *and* have to help me work besides."

"The point of our date wasn't to see a show, silly. It was to spend time with you. Let me come and help you. I don't know squat about arranging flowers, but I'm pretty good at following orders."

"You don't mind? You're sure?"

"Of course not. I'm about twenty minutes out. But why don't I go pick up Thai to-go and bring it to you."

"You are the best."

"I really am, aren't I?"

She smirked, but he'd won her heart with his offer.

"Do you need anything from the store? I can stop on my way over."

"Thanks, but I think I have everything I'll need. It's just not going to be exactly what the bride ordered. I just hope they'll understand. And of course, I'll cut my price."

"I'm sorry."

"It's just one of those things. Thanks, Tadhg. I mean it."

"Hey, what are friends for?"

"I love you." The three little words slipped out before she could stop them. Her breath caught. She'd been feeling it for a while now, but she hadn't meant to blurt it out like that. Not so soon. She wanted it to mean something when she told him for the first time.

Had those words scared him as much as the silence on his end scared her now?

"About that," he finally said. She couldn't tell if it was tenderness or regret in his tone. "I want to discuss that topic tonight, okay?"

"Of course...yes." *Oh, dear Lord, why can't I keep my mouth in check?*

SHE HEARD Tadhg's truck pull in and the butterflies in her belly went crazy. He climbed out, loaded down with bags from the Thai place.

She hurried to open the door for him, the spicy aromas of Pad Thai and Volcano Chicken making her mouth water. "I am so sorry about this, Tadhg. I feel awful for making you miss—"

"Shhh..." Putting a finger to his mouth, he dropped the bags beside the door, took her face in his hands, and kissed her long and sweet.

She couldn't help the way her body responded. Trembling and breathless, she pulled away and looked at him in awe.

"I love you too, sweet Emma," he whispered. He stroked her hair away from her forehead. "I should have said it first. I shouldn't have made you wait."

The warmth in his eyes was all the proof she needed.

"I was waiting for you to...say it first," she whispered. "But when you were so sweet to offer to help me, it just popped out. I couldn't stop it."

"That's the best way." He pulled her into his arms.

"What do you mean?"

"It means you really meant it."

"Of course, I did. I *do*. Oh, Tadhg, I do love you."

"And I love you." That cute impish grin he gave her so often came now. "Kind of cool how that works, isn't it?"

"Very cool." She tiptoed to give him another kiss—one far more chaste than the first one they'd shared. Her heart warmed just the same. "But we don't have time for kissing. It's going to take all night to fix this mess I'm in."

He gave her a deadpan look. "So romantic."

She giggled and took his hand. "Come on. Let's get this show on the road. We can talk while we work."

He lifted one eyebrow. "Can we kiss while we work?"

"Maybe a little."

"Then I'm in. But—can we eat first? I'm starving."

"Yes, of course. Let's feed you."

This night was turning out so wonderfully different than she'd imagined.

Chapter Twenty-Four

Emma looked up from the roll of ribbon she was cutting and smiled. Across the dining room table from her, Tadhg's face was a mask of concentration—a very handsome mask—as he wound green floral tape around the bunch of flowers she'd put together for a bridesmaid's bouquet. His work was meticulous and careful and oh, how she loved that he was here at her table. She remembered back to that first night he'd come for leftover lasagna, and she'd dared to imagine what it might be like to have him in her life, in this house, and she felt like a dream might be coming true.

She stripped leaves and put another bouquet together—tomorrow's bride had seven bridesmaids!—then trimmed the ends with secateurs before handing the arrangement off to Tadhg. All but four of the vases of flowers had frozen beyond repair. They'd managed to harvest enough blooms to replace the damaged ones, but her garden was looking pretty sparse now. She'd be lucky if there were enough new blossoms by next week to supply her booth at the farmers market, but at least she hadn't had to spend a nickel on grocery store flowers.

And she'd never had so much fun picking from her garden. Tadhg had shed his jacket, rolled up the sleeves of his white dress shirt, and they'd both kicked off their shoes and gotten to work—but not before Tadhg captured selfies of the two of them with his phone. He'd persuaded her to pose for some portraits in the garden too. "Look at you, all dressed up and looking beautiful with no place to go," he'd said.

He made her *feel* beautiful, so she followed his direction and posed, standing with her head bent to smell a bouquet, sitting cross-legged in front of the jasmine bushes, and walking through a field of cosmos. She hadn't looked closely at the pictures yet, but from the thumbnails she'd seen on his screen, she thought they might even work for a much-needed update to her website.

She honestly wasn't sure how she would have made it if he hadn't offered to help. When she suggested that she should share her proceeds from the job with him, he assured her the stolen kisses were payment enough.

And oh...those kisses. A lifetime of them wouldn't be enough.

They talked and flirted while they worked, with Tadhg leaning over her shoulder to see how the floral tape was supposed to be wound or how to secure the floral pins in the ribbon wrap, kissing her cheek before he went back to his side of the table.

He held up a finished bouquet for her to inspect. "Does this one meet your approval?"

"Turn it full-circle." She inspected his work. "You're going to put me out of a job."

"Well, I doubt that. I wouldn't have a clue about making the flowers look decent before wrapping them, but I didn't do too bad on this part."

"I'm having my book club here in September to make flower arrangements before our book discussion. Maybe you could come and teach them how to wrap ribbon," she teased.

"I think I'll pass, but thanks." He reached for the scissors and trimmed a frayed ribbon edge before folding it over to pin. "Hey, speaking of books, you'll be happy to know that I am reading a novel."

She feigned shock. "What a waste of time!"

He laughed.

"I'm enjoying it...I think."

"You think? What are you reading?"

"C.S. Lewis. *Till We Have Faces.*"

"You're ambitious."

"Yeah. It was kind of hard to get into at first but I'm about halfway through and I think I'll finish it."

"Oh, I can't stand to read halfway through a book and not finish it. If I invest fifty pages, even if it stinks, I'll at least skim to the end."

"Talk about a waste of time."

"I know." She wrinkled her nose. "But I just hate to be a quitter."

"That's admirable, I guess." He hesitated in a way that made her look up at him. "At the risk of bringing up a painful topic, a scene I read last night reminded me of your...*situation.*"

She laid the secateurs on the table and studied him. "It did? With the whole DNA thing? Why?"

He slid the bouquet he'd been working on in the bucket of water, pulled his phone from his pocket and scrolled.

"Are you reading the e-book version?"

"No. You saw my bookshelves. I like the real thing."

"Me too."

"No, the e-book was free so I got it to read on my lunch break. Not that I ever have time for anything but snarfing down a burger."

"So, which part reminded you of me?" She held her breath, not wanting to spoil the magic the evening had held thus far.

"Have you read it?"

"No. But I liked his Narnia books. I didn't discover them until I was in high school though."

"I liked them too. This one is a lot different though. More..."—he shrugged—"literary, I guess? The scene is between two sisters, Psyche and Orual—kind of a Cinderella and ugly stepsister situation. There's a secret that's causing a huge rift between them." He looked up from his phone. "Sound familiar?"

"*Too* familiar." She waited.

He scrolled on his phone, searching for the right place. "Here it is. This is Orual talking to her sister." He read aloud. "'You have a secret from me... No, don't turn away from me. Did you think I would try to press or conjure it out of you? Never that. Friends must be free. My tormenting you to find it would build a worse barrier between us than your hiding it. ... There, do not weep. I shall not cease to love you if you have a hundred secrets.'" Tadhg set his phone on the table but kept his head bowed.

The passage, especially that last line, moved her to tears. *I shall not cease to love you if you have a hundred secrets.* Oh, Mom... She didn't even try to hide the tears or to wipe her damp cheeks.

When he looked up at her, his expression turned to distress. "Oh, Emma. I didn't mean to make you cry." He scooted his chair back and came around to wrap his arms around her from behind. "I'm sorry."

"No... Will you read it again?"

He went back to his chair and read, slower this time, then scrolled again and tapped a link on the screen. "There's an annotation that says: 'This quote captures Orual's internal struggle when she recognizes that her desire to know the secret at all costs is creating a barrier between them. Her statement about friends needing to be free underscores her realization that true intimacy requires respect for the other's freedom, even when it involves secrets. The quote is a powerful exploration of love, jealousy, and the necessity of trust and freedom within relationships.'"

She swiped at the tears and gave him as much of a smile as she could muster. "You just had to go and read a novel."

He laughed. "I promise I wasn't looking for something to hit you over the head with. But this sure reminded me of you. And your mom. I figure with all the Bible-thumping I did that night, you've probably had about enough lectures from me."

She shook her head. "No, Tadhg. It was just what I needed to hear. I think I've known for a while now that I'm going to have to lay down this awful need to know—if I don't want to lose my Mom. And I don't. I miss her—" Her voice cracked.

He reached across the table and took her hands in his, and they sat that way for a few minutes. Finally, he looked up at the clock on the wall and whispered, "Did you know it's after midnight?"

She gave a little gasp. "Go home. I can finish up here. In the morning even. You don't need to stay."

"What if I *want* to? The two of us can whip this out in half the time you could."

She desperately wanted him to stay. "If you're sure."

He nodded and took the bouquet he'd been working on from the bucket, dried the stems, and started wrapping the ribbon around them the way she'd shown him.

They worked without talking for a while until Emma shook her head. "I'm just so impressed you read a novel."

He chuckled. "Well, I haven't finished it yet, so don't be too impressed."

Chapter Twenty-Five

Tadhg drove slowly along the streets that snaked through Georgetown, watching for house numbers as he went. He'd had to do some serious detective work to find the address, but thankfully, Emma had unwittingly revealed most of the details he needed in the course of their late night conversations last night.

He smiled, thinking of the kisses they'd shared. They'd moved to a new level and it seemed so right. After they'd eaten, they foraged for replacement flowers in the garden, still in their theater clothes. Emma had been so playful and happy, despite the stress of the flower fiasco. They'd taken selfies and then he snapped some photos of her in the garden. She looked like a princess, and her garden had made a stunning backdrop at the golden hour. It gave him an idea for a present for her birthday.

But the thing that touched him most about the pictures he'd taken was the love that shone in her smile. A smile only for him. What they'd declared for each other last night was written in the sparkle of her eyes and the glow on her face.

Today, despite having the best intentions, he felt guilty that Emma didn't know what he was up to while she was distributing wedding flowers. But hopefully, he would give her the one birthday present she wanted most, and then he could tell her everything. No secrets between them ever again.

He was getting close according to the house numbers. There it was on the right. The house was grander than he'd expected and set back from the street with an impressive yard dotted with massive live oaks. He parked on the street and walked up the driveway to the front door.

He heard the faint chime of the doorbell from inside. Wiping sweaty palms on his khakis, he waited, rehearsing his plea. The door opened and an attractive middle-aged woman appeared, looking puzzled.

"Can I help you?"

"Hi. My name is Tadhg McKay. Are you Emma Fiori's mom?"

The woman put a hand to her throat and alarm shone in her eyes. "Is Emma okay?"

Tadhg held up a hand. "Yes, yes. I'm sorry. I should have said that first. She's fine. She's doing flowers for a wedding on the island today. I'm Tadhg, Emma's friend."

Her mother waited for him to explain further.

"Emma doesn't know I'm here, but— Could I speak with you for a few minutes?"

"Just a minute. Let me get my husband, please." She disappeared into the house and he heard the door lock behind her. He didn't blame her, but when several minutes went by, he wondered if he'd been ghosted.

But a minute later, the door opened again and Emma's mom stood there with a man about her age. He extended a hand. "I'm Bill Chambers. Caroline said you're Emma's friend?"

Tadhg shook his hand. "Yes. Emma and I are dating." He turned to Caroline. "Could I talk to you"—he held up a handful of fingers—"just for five minutes?"

She seemed to leap into action. "Of course. Please come in."

When they were seated in a tidy, well-appointed living room, Bill asked, "Can I get you something to drink."

"No, that's okay. But thank you. I won't stay long."

They both looked at him expectantly. "Emma has told me about what's going on and that you had asked for a break from her. She's—"

"Now, that's not exactly what I said." Caroline sat forward on the sofa. Her husband put a hand on her back as if to calm her.

"I might have misunderstood," Tadhg said quickly, "but the bottom line is, she's afraid to reach out to you. For fear you'll reject her again." Tadhg had thought long and hard how to best accomplish his goal without betraying Emma. "She's missing you terribly. She's been processing things, and I think she understands that she may never get the answers she wants—about her birth parents. I came to ask if you would consider seeing Emma on her birthday? She doesn't feel much like celebrating—because she doesn't think you will be there. I wanted to do something to cheer her up and I know there's nothing she'd love more than to see you. If...if she would promise not to push you to give her answers, would you consider coming to a birthday party Tuesday night?"

Caroline closed her eyes and seemed to consider his request. Though her hair was silver gray, Emma's mother still looked youthful and attractive. Something about her facial expressions and the way she held herself reminded him uncannily of Emma. He made a note to tell Emma that—when the time was right. It was obvious that nurture created as many similarities as nature.

For a minute, he let himself picture a future Emma when she was the age her mother was now. Emma with silver hair but her skin still peaches and cream. He liked what he saw in his mind's eye and—

Caroline's voice interrupted his daydreams. "Yes. We'll come. And...you don't need to extract any promises from her. I'll take that one step at a time." Again, she turned to her husband. "Is Tuesday night okay for you, Bill?"

"Of course. I'll make it work. Where is the party?"

Tadhg gave an awkward laugh. "She doesn't know it yet, but it will probably be at her house. My apartment isn't really big enough. I thought I would surprise her, but maybe that isn't a good idea? I don't know... You know her better than I do. Obviously."

Caroline seemed to warm to that. "I think a surprise party would be wonderful. And can I bring the cake? I'll make her favorite."

"That...that would be perfect." He hardly knew how to respond to such a positive reply. He'd rehearsed all kinds of speeches to convince Emma's mom if she refused, but he hadn't thought how he'd reply if she said yes. "Just come to Emma's house around six. I'll take care of supper. And— Maybe it would be best if it's just the four of us. Under the circumstances."

Caroline's forehead furrowed. "Circumstances?"

"Oh. I didn't mean... I just think it will be a very emotional time—*happy* emotions," he added quickly. "When she sees that you're there. That might be awkward for her if others are around."

"Of course." Her inflection was so like Emma's. "That's so thoughtful of you... Was it...Tagg?"

He grinned. "It's Tadhg. Like Tiger." He spelled it for them and made the same jokes he'd made with Emma—and a thousand other people who couldn't figure out why T-A-D-H-G spelled Tiger-without-the-ER. He refrained from showing them his bicep. Maybe he'd bring that out at the birthday party.

"Thank you for coming, Tadhg." She looked at Bill with raised eyebrows, as if asking permission of some sort. He gave a nod of his chin and Caroline turned back to Tadhg. "I've been wrestling with this night and day. I...I'm considering telling Emma some of the details of her birth. I *can't* tell her everything, but like Bill says, what she's imagining—because I won't tell her *anything*—is probably worse than the parts I can't tell her. But do you think she's strong enough to hear some of the truth? Or has she accepted that I can't tell her, and maybe I should just let it go?"

A little bewildered, Tadhg started, "I think she's—"

"Caroline." Bill interrupted, putting an arm around his wife. In a mildly scolding voice, he said, "I thought you'd made up your mind."

She sat up straight and breathed in deeply. "Yes. Yes, I have. Okay. Unless you think there's a reason I shouldn't, Tadhg, I'm going to give her some of the details. They...they won't be easy to hear, and there are some parts of her story that simply aren't mine to tell, but like Bill said, she has a right to know."

"I know she will be so grateful. But most of all, she'll just be so happy to see you again."

"Maybe I won't tell her *on* her birthday. I don't want to make it a bad memory for her. Every year. But I'll tell her soon. And I'll let her know that. Prepare her a little bit."

"Thank you." He risked reaching to touch her hand briefly. "Thank you so much." He pushed himself out of the overstuffed chair. "Well... I said five minutes and I think it's been more than ten."

"That's no problem." Bill rose and led the way to the door.

"We'll try to eat around six thirty if that works for you."

"Of course, we'll be there. And don't forget I'm making the cake."

"Thank you. I appreciate that. Oh, and here's my card, in case you need to get in touch. Or you could just call Emma. But that would spoil the surprise." He slipped a business card from his wallet and handed it to Bill.

"We'll see you Tuesday night," Bill said. With his back to his wife, he mouthed an emphatic *thank-you* to Tadhg.

His truck might as well be flying along I-95 all the way back to the island.

"You're doing the right thing, Caroline." Bill faced her and put his hands on her shoulder.

"Am I? I keep thinking the truth might be even worse than not knowing for her."

"Emma is strong. Everything will be okay. She deserves the truth."

She fell into his embrace and wept. "Please keep telling me that."

"Sweetheart, you did a heroic and noble thing. You gave your daughter life! A wonderful life. You have nothing to fear. She will understand. It might take a while to wrap her head around things, but she'll manage. Just like you would if you were in her shoes."

Oh, how she loved this man God had given her after those sad years since Tony's death. She wasn't sure Tony could have handled this situation any better than Bill had—and Tony had loved Emma more than any father could love a daughter.

An onslaught of memories came and she let them come, hoping she could find peace in remembering. They'd still been making wedding plans the night she found out. And when she first told him that she wanted to adopt the baby, he was adamant. "That's crazy, babe! We'd barely be home from our honeymoon. I understand how hard it would be to know someone else was adopting the baby and that you might never see it again, but—"

"That's just it, Tony. They're not considering adoption anymore."

"What? They're going to raise the baby themselves?"

"No. You don't understand. She's having an abortion." Her voice broke. "She told me she made an appointment this morning."

His face fell. "How can they do that? How can they even think about it."

She shook her head. "I don't know. I begged her not to, and when she wouldn't listen I told her—"

"You told her we'd take the baby? How is that any different than someone else adopting the baby?"

"Because she said she couldn't stand the thought of not knowing where it was."

"Don't they know about open adoptions, Caroline. They could have a relationship with the adoptive parents and the baby—"

But she was already shaking her head. "No. She's heard too many horror stories about those. That's what she said."

He'd sighed and bowed his head then, and that was the moment she knew he would say yes. It wasn't that they didn't want children. Tony always said he wanted six, though she didn't think he was serious about that. But now was not the time for a baby. Not like this."

Finally, he raised his head and looked at her with...not defeat, exactly. Maybe resignation was a better word. "Okay, my love. I guess we're having a baby. But what will we tell people?"

"She's due in June. Eight months after our wedding. It's not that unusual."

"And what? You're going to wear maternity clothes and pretend it's our baby?" He shook his head.

"She won't let us tell anyone. That's her condition. She's going to"—she formed quote marks with her fingers—"'visit' her sister once she starts showing. I'll just...I'll lay low for a few months before the birth."

"I'm not going to lie," Tony said. "About any of this."

"Even if it means saving a life? She'll go through with it—the abortion. I know she will, Tony. Something's changed with her and she...she's not herself. It's the only way! Please..."

It had been decided then. That night. They would adopt the baby, raise it as their own. And promise that they would never, ever, ever tell anyone the truth. Not the child, especially. And Caroline would never tell Emma that part—that her birth mother had wanted—planned—to abort her. Bill was the only one who knew that part and only because "the two shall become one" meant that he was part of her and telling him wouldn't be breaking her promise. It would have been a story of victory if the birth parents had been strangers. But they hadn't. Far from it.

Part of her wished her parents were here to help her navigate this strange road. But a bigger part of her was grateful they weren't.

Things had been complicated between them after she and Tony adopted Emma. And if this was hard for her, *it would have been a thousand times harder for Mother and Dad.*

But she'd made a firm decision tonight, the second most difficult of her life, and she was going to carry through. The promise had been extracted from her and it had held her prisoner from that day forward. But Bill was right. The consequences weren't nearly as severe now that Emma was grown.

Unless Emma completely rejected her once she found out the truth.

Caroline shook herself from the memories. She had chosen a lesser of two evils and she would live with the aftermath. And pray that God would forgive her for going back on her word.

Chapter Twenty-Six

Tadhg knocked on the frame of Jillian's open door. "Good morning."

She looked up. "Hey, Tadhg. What's up?"

"I just wanted to remind you that I need to take off right at five tonight." He'd told her early last week, and reminded her again on Friday, but she sometimes had selective memory when it came to overtime.

"Yes. I wanted to talk to you about that." She motioned him to come in. "Close the door there, why don't you."

Adrenaline zipped through his veins. Was he about to get fired?

When he was seated, she came right to the point. "Brian won't be with us after Friday. He's missed too many days and it's costing us an arm and a leg to have everybody working so much overtime."

He gave an internal sigh. Okay, good. Not fired, but so much for the good money he was making with overtime.

"I've hired two new guys. One starts Monday and the other early in September. I'd like you to train them—and any other new hires from here on out."

"Sure. I don't mind doing that." He would actually enjoy it a great deal.

"It'll come with a small pay raise, of course. Not a ton of extra money, but it is a promotion and you'd be salaried with annual reviews. Frank and I have been talking, and we'd make your title Senior Technician-slash-Trainer, but of course during the times there's no one new to train, you'd be back in the field doing what you're doing now."

"Sure, I understand."

"That said, we've even been thinking about doing some training workshops for the current techs. You seem to be able to service more clients and have fewer customer complaints than anybody around here. Maybe you can teach these yahoos your ways."

He laughed. "I make no promises, but I can give it a shot." His mind was already reeling with ideas for revising the current training manuals and creating some video tutorials.

"I'll have papers for you to sign sometime this week. I'll let you know when we have everything drawn up."

Sensing her dismissal, he rose and extended a hand across her desk. "Thank you. I really appreciate this."

He was halfway out the door when Jillian called him back.

"Why don't you take off at four tonight. You've been burning the candle at both ends."

"Thanks. I appreciate that, Jillian. All of it."

He grabbed his gear and headed for his truck. It was the second time this week that his truck could fly.

EMMA MADE sweet tea and put it in the fridge, then she went to fluff the throw pillows for the third time in an hour. Tadhg had said he'd take care of everything and all she had to do was provide the venue and maybe something to drink. Oh, and flowers.

"You make it hard for a man to get you anything when flowers are off the table."

"I know but why pay a fortune, when I can pick a bigger, prettier vase full from my garden for nothing? Don't worry," she'd said. "I'll take care of the flowers."

She didn't have a clue what he had in mind, but as long as *he* was here to help her celebrate her birthday, that was all that really mattered. All day she'd pushed away thoughts of Mom. She wasn't sure she'd ever celebrated a birthday without her mother. Granted, there had been some sad ones—the year after Dad died, and the birthdays after her grandparents' deaths. But Mom had always been the one constant. The one friend she could count on, who would—

"Stop it." She jumped up, chiding herself. Her voice made Bud look up from his perch on the back of the sofa. She went to the cat and stroked his chin. "I wasn't talking to you, buddy. You just keep doing what you're doing."

Bud's motor kicked in, which almost made her cry again. He'd been a good little friend, too. Through thick and thin. Taking a deep breath, she walked away from the purring furball, lest the faucets turn on again. She'd spent far too long on her mascara for that.

She didn't want to ruin this evening Tadhg had planned with tears. That man was so sweet. She didn't deserve his love, and yet when he looked at her with such love in his eyes, all doubt was gone.

At five forty-five she pre-heated the oven as Tadhg had instructed. Finally, six o'clock rolled around and his truck came up the driveway. Emma watched through the front windows as he hopped out, went around to the passenger side, and extracted a large cardboard box.

She opened the door for him and he grinned and leaned over the box to kiss her. "Happy birthday, beautiful. I'll give you a proper kiss as soon as I get everything carried in."

"Let me help."

"Uh-uh. It's your birthday. You go sit down and get comfortable. I have a little prep to do before I can join you, but it won't take long. Is the oven hot?"

"It is." She giggled. She could get used to this being pampered business.

She watched from the sofa as he carried in boxes of food, festive paper goods, and finally, a long folding table. He went back to lock the truck, then came in and set to work. She heard him put something in the oven, then he set up the folding table in front of the living room windows and covered it with a lacy crocheted tablecloth.

"Look at you, all fancy," she teased. "That's really pretty. The tablecloth."

He glanced at her over one shoulder. "Izzy assured me you'd like it. She knit it herself."

"I think it's crocheted, but it's beautiful. I love it. Tell her thank you for her contribution to my party decorations."

He ignored her and went into the kitchen. She heard him opening drawers in search of utensils and tableware.

"Let me know if you need help finding anything," she shouted into the kitchen.

"Why don't you go wait on the loggia," he hollered back. "You're making me nervous."

"It's too hot out there right now. I'll be quiet. I promise."

She put her feet up on the sofa and basked in the sounds of him in the kitchen. A few minutes later he came back to the living room and started arranging things on the table. One of the vases of flowers she'd arranged on the left end, a short stack of pretty paper plates and birthday napkins, and half a dozen colorful plastic cups. She was thankful for those limited numbers. For a minute, she'd been afraid he'd invited a bunch of their friends—neither of which knew each other. But it looked like the party might be just the two of them, and that was fine by her.

She was mildly disappointed to see that there wasn't a birthday cake on the table. As long as she could remember, Mom had always made her famous Peach Caramel Pound Cake. But maybe there was a store-bought cake in the kitchen or the fridge. And even if there wasn't, she couldn't possibly feel more cherished for all Tadhg had done to make her day special.

He added a lavender envelope with her name on it and a beautifully wrapped gift box to the table. The thin box bore a sticker with a jeweler's logo and was the shape that might hold a necklace or bracelet.

After a few minutes of puttering at the table—with her doing her best to keep her vow of silence—he picked up a large, flat box he'd leaned near the front door, and brought it over to the sofa. "Okay, this is part of the decorations, but it's also a present, so you get to open this before...we eat. Sorry I didn't wrap it but—" He shrugged.

She swung her legs to the floor and straightened. He watched while she untaped the box and slid out a canvas. He set the cardboard box aside, then took the canvas from her and turned it around so she could see the front.

Tears sprang to her eyes. "Oh, Tadhg, I love it!"

The gallery-wrapped canvas was a print of one of the photos he'd taken that day in the garden, but she hadn't been aware he'd gotten this perspective. She was walking away from the camera through the stand of cosmos, her outstretched palms brushing the feathery leaves, and the rest of the garden in front of her bathed in golden light, but out of focus in a way that gave the whole portrait a dreamy quality.

"I thought you might." He looked pretty proud of himself.

"You couldn't have captured the garden better. And *me*. I don't usually like photos of myself, but this is perfect. But how did you get the print done so soon?"

He rolled his eyes. "Let me tell you, *that* was the hard part. I just picked it up from the post office on my way over. It's a good thing I got off early today."

"Well, I couldn't love it more." She craned her neck toward

the table he'd set up and cleared her throat pointedly. "Did I see another gift?"

"Oh, no. That one has to wait until after dinner."

"Well, then, let's eat."

His gaze cut to the front door as if he was expecting someone. So maybe it wasn't just the two of them. "First, I have something to tell you." He slid onto the sofa beside her.

She pressed a palm against his chest. "First, you said you'd give me a proper kiss as soon as you got everything in the house. I'm still waiting."

Without a word he took her in his arms and gave her the most proper kiss she'd ever received. And then one that wasn't quite so proper." Giggling, but also sensing things were getting a little too close to "improper," she pulled away. "So, what was it you wanted to tell me?"

"I got a promotion this week." His chest puffed out. "It's not a ton more money, but it's salaried. I'll be training new hires on-the-job, and maybe even doing some in-house workshops."

"Tadhg! That's fantastic. By workshops, do you mean the kind where you'd be teaching?" Something told her he hadn't quite put two and two together yet.

"That and maybe making some tutorial videos and updating the—" He looked at her and she could see the moment it struck him.

He smacked his forehead and his jaw dropped. "Duh. No wonder I'm so happy about the promotion. Seriously, Emma, I hadn't even thought about that. That I'd be teaching."

Tears were close and she couldn't remember ever feeling so proud of another person. "Just look what God has done, Tadhg. I am so proud of you!"

That brought another bout of hugs and kisses and *I love yous*. It was going to be hard to keep things "proper" between them. They were going to have to find things to do to keep busy when they were together. In that frame of reference, she pushed away again. "I love you and I'm proud of you, but I'm starving. Can we eat yet?"

He checked his phone for the time and looked perplexed. "Not quite yet. Let's wait just a few more minutes."

"Who else is coming, Tadhg. You're not fooling me."

"Just hold your pretty little horses. You'll see."

For a brief moment, she let herself hope that Mom was the mystery guest. There was nothing she'd love more than for her mom to walk through that front door. But even if she surprised Emma, Tadhg would have no way of knowing that. And she wasn't sure this was how she wanted him and Mom to meet for the first time.

She rose from the sofa. "Well, let me get us something to drink, okay?"

"Sure. I saw there was tea in the fridge. Why don't you pour a couple of glasses." He checked his phone again.

This time, it looked like he clicked on the Messages app. Something was definitely afoot.

He slipped his phone back in his pocket, seeming distracted. "Do you think it's cool enough to go out on the loggia yet?"

"Sure. Let me go put the umbrellas up."

As she opened the door, his phone rang. He looked at the screen and smiled, his shoulders sagging with relief. She quickly went outside so he wouldn't see that she was watching.

She could hear him talking to someone through the open screen but couldn't make out what he was saying. But if she had to guess, his tone sounded like someone had canceled on him. She wouldn't be sad to spend the evening just with him.

Through the sheer living room curtains, she could just see his shadow moving inside. And then he stopped in front of her birthday table. He stood there for so long that she almost went in to see what was keeping him. But before she could rise, he came through the door.

"Emma. I'm so sorry." His face was drained of color. "It's

your mom. Something has happened. You need to come with me."

Chapter Twenty-Seven

Like an automaton, Tadhg turned off the oven, pulled out the pan of burritos and set them on the top of the stove. They were too hot to put in the refrigerator but that couldn't be helped.

He turned to find Emma standing in the doorway, shoes on, purse on her shoulder, watching him with fear in her eyes.

"I got the oven. Is there anything else we need to turn off before we go?"

"No, I got Bud inside and he has food and water." She swatted his questions away. "What is going on, Tadhg. You said it's Mom?"

"Let's just go. I'll explain everything in the car." He tried to think how he could possibly soften this blow. At least he'd be able to tell her that her mother had planned to be at her party.

He opened the passenger door and shut it carefully once she was settled. Then he went around to climb behind the wheel. Once they were on the road toward Savannah, he turned to her, praying he wouldn't have to pull over.

"That was Bill who called. Your mom is in the ER."

"Mom?" She gasped. "What happened?"

"They don't know for sure, but they think she may have had a stroke."

"A stroke? How can that even be? She's only fifty-six."

"I don't know. I wish I had more answers. But Bill wanted us to come." He didn't tell her that Bill told him Caroline had been unresponsive when he found her on the floor in their kitchen. She'd apparently hit her head when she fell and there was swelling from that. It didn't sound good.

Tadhg took Emma's hand in his and squeezed. "Let's pray for her, okay?"

She nodded and bowed her head, her shoulders shaking.

He kept his eyes on the road ahead. The last thing they needed was an accident. "God, we don't know what's going on, but Emma's mom needs healing. Please help the doctors figure out what's wrong, and bring her back to full health. Please, Lord."

"In Jesus's name," she whispered. She seemed a bit calmer when she looked up.

Maybe this was a good time to tell her. "Your mom planned to come to your party today. She was bringing your birthday cake."

She looked at him with eyes wide. "How do you know that?"

He smiled softly. "I talked to her. A few days ago. They—"

"What? When did you talk to her? Mom called you? How?"

"Shhh." He touched her arm to quiet her. "No, I...contacted her and Bill. Your mom was missing you as much as you've been missing her. They were excited about coming to your party."

She sucked in a breath and put a hand to her mouth. "You don't think they were on their way over when it happened? Oh, Tadhg. I could never forgive myself if—"

"No." He shushed her. "They hadn't left yet. She was still at home when it happened. Bill told me they were getting ready to leave." He prayed she wouldn't ask for more details.

She was quiet for a dozen miles and he didn't try to make conversation.

And then she straightened. "Oh, Tadhg... When I was at their house, that day I went through Mom's desk, I…saw some pills in the medicine cabinet. Mom's name was on the bottle. She never said anything about it. And we talked about everything. That's not the kind of thing she would keep from me." She looked at her lap. "At least not before. Do you think she's sick. I mean really sick?"

He patted her knee gently. "Let's not go there. Let's see what Bill and the doctors know first."

She nodded and went quiet again.

His truck wasn't flying down the Interstate today. The trip to Memorial's ER in Savannah seemed to take an eternity. When he pulled into the emergency room parking lot, he thought to drop Emma off at the entrance before he parked the truck, but looking at her beside him, her face pale, fingers still trembling, he changed his mind.

Thankfully, he was able to park close and it was a short walk to the entrance. He put an arm around her shoulders as they entered through the doors together.

At the reception desk, Emma seemed surprised when he asked for Bill and Caroline Chambers by name. He desperately needed to tell her that he'd gone to talk to them, but there were more important things to worry about right now.

The receptionist informed them that Caroline had been admitted to the ICU and directed them to an elevator down the corridor. He didn't know what to expect but tried to mentally prepare for comforting Emma through the worst.

Bill must have seen them coming, because he appeared from a doorway and hurried toward them. "Emma."

"Is she okay? What happened?" All the same questions she'd asked him after Bill called.

Bill kept his voice low and that seemed to calm Emma, but she kept glancing toward the door he'd exited, knowing her mom was in there.

"They're running some tests, still trying to figure out exactly what happened, but they think she had a stroke. She came to for a little bit in the ambulance, but right now she's sedated."

"Did you talk to her? In the ambulance?"

He shook his head. "Not really. I think she knew me, but she was having trouble speaking. It's one of the things that made them think she's had a stroke. Dr. Barlowe won't be in until morning, so we probably won't know anything tonight."

"Can I see her?" Emma's voice splintered.

"Yes. For just a few minutes. They're limiting visitors, at least for tonight. Oh—" He sucked in a breath and gave her a weak smile. "I almost forgot. Happy birthday, Emma."

"Thank you. Not exactly how I wanted to celebrate."

Bill agreed with a nod. "I assume Tadhg told you we had planned to be at your party?"

She nodded. "He told me on the way here."

Bill shot Tadhg an apologetic smile. "Hope I didn't spoil the surprise. But hey listen, Emma, your birthday cake is in the fridge at home. Why don't you go get it and take it home with you."

"Um... I don't have a key anymore."

"Oh, I'm sorry. Of course. Well, I could give you the garage code."

Emma waved him off. "It's okay. I don't much feel like celebrating."

"I understand. Do you want to stay at the house tonight? I assume you'll want to come back and see her in the morning."

She looked at Tadhg with a question in her expression.

"I really can't miss work tomorrow, but I could bring you over again after work. Maybe we could drive your car and I can take a cab back?"

"No, Tadhg. You don't need to do that. That'd cost a fortune. I'll just drive back in the morning." She turned to Bill. "I know they won't let me stay with her in the room, but if it's okay with you, I'll drive back tomorrow and maybe stay at your house tomorrow night.—depending on how she's doing. I'll have to come home to take care of the garden every couple of days, but I'm not too excited about driving back and forth every day."

"Let's hope there aren't very many days to worry about."

Emma nodded emphatically, then turned to Tadhg. "I'm going to go see her. I won't be long. And then if she's...stable, we can go back to the island."

He put an arm around her. "I'll be right here. Take as long as you want."

Concern shadowed Bill's face. "Did Tadhg tell you about her—"

"I only said that they thought it was a stroke." Tadhg hugged her. "I'm sorry. I should have told you. Your mom hit her head when she fell, so there's some swelling and bruising." He turned to Bill. "Did I get that right?"

"Yes. The swelling has already gone down some, but she still looks pretty rough, Emma, so just be prepared."

Tadhg planted a kiss in her hair before he let her go and whispered a prayer for strength.

She followed Bill, looking like she was going to the gallows. Tadhg's heart broke for her.

THE ROOM WAS DIM, which only emphasized the chaos of blinking lights and beeping monitors. Mom looked so small in the hospital bed. Her eyes were closed and she was hooked up to an IV and an oxygen mask. One thing that wasn't small was her head. The whole left side of her face was twice as big as the other and her left eye was starting to turn black and blue.

Emma was afraid to touch her for fear of startling her or setting off some alarm. But Bill came beside her and took Mom's hand. No response, but he spoke to her as if she could hear every word.

"Caroline, Emma is here."

He took Emma's hand and gently placed it where his had been. The warmth of Mom's skin comforted her...at least it proved she was alive.

"Mom? Mom, it's me. Emma. Can you hear me?"

Again, no response. Not so much as an eyelid twitching or a finger pulsing. She'd never felt so helpless. She made the mistake of glancing back at Bill. He was weeping, his shoulders shaking like an earthquake. She lost it then and put her head down and sobbed. Bill put a strong hand on her back and guided her away from the bed.

When they were out of Mom's sight he whispered, "She's going to be okay. We have to believe that. In the meantime, the nurses said to assume that she can hear everything we say, so let's try to hold it together for her sake, okay?"

She nodded and swallowed hard, gathering her composure.

At Mom's bedside, Bill leaned close and spoke close to her ear. "It's Emma's birthday, Caroline? Did you remember? How many is it, Emma? I've forgotten."

"Twenty-eight," she squeaked, struggling to hold it together.

"So, how was your party? I heard Tadhg planned quite a night."

Seriously? *Don't make me do this, Bill.* "He...he did. He made dinner and decorated the table." She told him about the canvas Tadhg had done from the photos in the garden." She did her best to sound normal and played along though her heart wasn't in it.

"I'm so sorry we couldn't make it, honey." Bill's voice was more natural and conversational now. "We'll be sure you get the birthday cake your mom made."

"Thank you. I can't wait to taste it." She leaned closer to the bed and took her mom's hand. "Thanks so much for baking it for me, Mom."

Nothing. Absolutely no response. If not for the monitors blipping her pulse rate and heartbeat, and the annoying *whoosh whoosh* of the oxygen machine, the room would have been in complete silence.

Chapter Twenty-Eight

Emma stared down at her mother's face, praying under her breath. It had been three days with no changes. Mostly because they'd been sedating Mom, but Bill told Emma that they planned to begin weaning her off of the meds this weekend. It scared her to think of them taking her off of medications that were keeping her peaceful and calm. They'd warned that Mom might be frightened and agitated coming off the meds.

Worse, once she was fully conscious, they'd know what they were dealing with.

Bill came to stand beside Mom's bed. Tenderly, he touched the bruises on her forehead. "Part of the problem is the swelling caused by the fall, so they're kind of dealing with two different issues. At least that's what I understood the nurse to say last night."

"You were there when she fell?"

"I didn't *see* her fall, and I don't know how long she'd been on the floor when I found her, but I could tell she'd hit her head. Those granite counters are like hitting cement."

She winced, imagining how painful it must have been. "But it wasn't just the fall, right?"

"No, they're almost certain she had a stroke and that's what caused her to fall."

"Was Mom having symptoms? I mean, was there any warning at all that she might have a stroke?" She hadn't admitted to them that she'd snooped in their medicine cabinet, and this wasn't the time to confess that, but she fished for information anyway. If Bill became suspicious about why she was prying, she would tell him the truth.

"No, not really," Bill said. "She probably told you that she was diagnosed with high blood pressure a while back. But they had her on medication for that and it was keeping her blood pressure right where the doctor wanted it."

"Do you think— Could it have been the stress over...my DNA test and all that? Did the doctor say anything about stress causing this?" It was an unfair question, but she needed to know.

Bill didn't hesitate. "No, Emma. Don't even go there. Not for one minute. All of that mess was stressful for your mom, of course, just as it was stressful for you. But don't you dare blame yourself for this.

She dipped her head. "It's kind of hard not to."

Dr. Barlowe strolled into the room, clipboard in hand. "How's she doing today?"

He'd addressed his question to Emma, but she deferred to Bill, since she'd only been here a few minutes.

"Not much different. The nurse said they were weaning her off the sedatives, but she's still pretty out of it."

"It takes time," the doctor said, glancing at the charts. "They just gave her the first reduced dosages at noon. It'll be gradual over the next few days. Some people come out of it faster than others. And don't be alarmed if she's still pretty unresponsive or even agitated once she does come out of it."

The rest of what the doctor said went over her head. Or maybe she just didn't *want* to understand. She just wanted her mom back. The way she'd been before. Before the stroke, before the DNA test.

Emma parked in the now-familiar parking lot at the hospital and gave Tadhg a resigned look before they headed into the building. She had to psych herself up before opening those doors every time. She'd stayed over at Bill's several nights during the early days of Mom's hospitalization, but when there was so little change, she'd stayed home and just made the hour and a half drive each afternoon, then drove home while the sun set. But that meant that often she was weeding and watering the garden in the dark.

She was grateful that Tadhg had offered to come with her tonight. He'd offered to drive his truck, but she was spending a small fortune in gas going back and forth, and it wasn't fair for him to have to bear that cost.

But she couldn't stand the thought of not seeing Mom for at least a little while each day. And she wanted to be there when Mom finally woke up. The doctor had said that was when they would begin to know what they were dealing with and how severely the stroke had affected her.

The nurses had been great, but Emma wasn't overly fond of Dr. Barlowe, mostly because he didn't seem to offer them a lot of hope. His best-case scenarios involved physical and cognitive rehabilitation therapy and even long-term nursing care. Maybe he just didn't want to get their hopes up in case the worst happened, but she needed a dose of hope. And she thought Bill did too.

Tadhg had come with her last Thursday night, too, but he'd waited outside Mom's room. "I'd rather see her when she's well," he said. That was the kind of encouragement she needed, and she was grateful for Tadhg McKay—and frustrated that their budding love had been put on hold. Oh, he was sweet and tender with her and kissed her goodnight with longing in his touch. But they talked about little besides Mom's condition and what the schedule was for going to visit her. She would be glad when they could get back to normal.

She left Tadhg in the waiting room and entered Mom's room. Bill was already there, sitting by her bed. "How is she?"

He only shrugged in reply. The oxygen mask was off and Mom was restless. But maybe that was a good sign.

"Has she opened her eyes at all?"

"Just for a minute. But every time they try to dial back the sedatives, she gets agitated and then her blood pressure skyrockets." He spoke in low tones, a reminder that Mom could very well hear everything they said.

She lowered her voice accordingly. "Is it normal for it to go on this long?"

"It's different for every patient. To quote Dr. Barlowe."

Emma rolled her eyes, not caring if Bill knew how she felt about the man.

He rose wearily. "I'm going to go get something to drink. I'll let you have some time alone with her."

"Thanks, Bill. Tadhg's with me tonight. He's in the waiting room." She nodded toward the door.

"Oh, good. I'll see if he wants to walk down and get something to drink with me. We won't leave the building."

She was grateful for that. She lived in fear of her mom waking up when she was alone with her. What would she do if Mom was...not herself? Taking a deep breath, she approached the bed, doing her best to sound cheerful and unconcerned. "Hey, Mom. How's it going today? Bill says you're giving them a hard time."

She took her mom's hand and held it. They'd never been very physically affectionate with each other, but she'd relished Mom's touch this past week. And she'd read that it was good for stroke patients to be touched and talked to.

"Can you hear me, Mom? Bill went down to get something to drink but he'll be right back. Tadhg went with him. He drove me tonight." She doubted Mom remembered who Tadhg was, but if she had to be here much longer, Emma wanted Tadhg to meet her.

"Mom? Can you hear me?" she asked again.

Her mother tossed her head from side to side and made some guttural sounds.

"That's it. Can you wake up, Mom?" Maybe she just needed a little encouragement. "Open your eyes."

Maybe she was just imagining it, but she thought her eyelids twitched a little, as if she was making an effort.

Emma watched her closely for several minutes, trying to think of things to talk about. These one-sided conversations were painful. "I did flowers for a wedding you would have loved a couple weeks ago. The bride had seven bridesmaids. Can you imagine?"

Mom cried out and Emma gasped. Mom yelled again and this time it sounded like she was trying to talk, but it wasn't any language Emma had ever heard.

"What did you say, Mom? Can you say it again?"

A few syllables, but they were gibberish. Mom's eyes were still closed but she was clearly trying to open them and becoming very agitated in the process.

"That's it. Open your eyes. Can you hear me?"

Another string of gibberish. Emma felt panicked. Did this mean she'd lost her ability to speak? That was one of the most devastating damages a stroke could leave behind. What if she could never talk to her mother again? What if Mom's secret had been lost forever?

"Let me get a nurse, okay? I'll be right back. I love you, Mom," she said, almost as an afterthought. In case... She couldn't finish the sentence, even in her mind.

SHE FELT like she was underwater. Everything was wavering, blurry, like when three-year-old Emma had smeared sunscreen on her sunglasses that day at the beach. She'd liked to never have gotten that greasy stuff off of her lenses.

Emma was here. In the room. Some kind of hospital. Was

Emma sick? No. She was walking around the room, looking out the window, pacing. Stop it, girl. You're making me nervous. Why was her daughter ignoring her?

Her eyelids felt so heavy. She could hardly keep them open. She tried to lift her hand to wave at Emma, but her arm was heavy like her eyelids.

Someone else came in the room. A nurse. Why was Emma in the hospital?

"Caroline? Caroline?" The nurse rubbed her arm. "Can you hear me?"

Emma came over and stood beside the nurse.

"Why are you here, Emma?" Wait. Who said that? Someone was talking gibberish. No, it was her. She wasn't making any sense. She said the words again. "Emma, Emma... Why are you here?" But the words didn't come out right. They were right in her head, but when they came out of her mouth, they were all jumbled up. All wrong.

The nurse stepped back and Emma leaned over her. What? It wasn't Emma in the hospital bed. It must be her. *"Why am I here, Emma? Get me out of this bed."*

"What, Mom? What are you trying to say? Can you say it again?"

What was wrong with that girl? Why couldn't she make her understand? Was this some kind of joke? Well, it wasn't funny. "Stop that right now, Emma June! Why am I here?"

"It's okay, Mom. Just rest. Don't try to talk. It's okay. We'll try again later."

"Try what?"

"Shhh. It's okay, Mom." Tears welled in her eyes.

Why was she crying? "Just answer my question." That gibberish again. In her own voice. Or was someone mimicking her?

Chapter Twenty-Nine

Bill appeared around the corner in the small waiting room where Tadhg sat. He carried two sweating cans of Coca-Cola and held one out to Tadhg.

He rose, took the drink, and shook Bill's free hand. "How's she doing today?"

"About the same. Emma said you were here, but I must have just missed you."

"I was in the restroom. Thanks for the Coke."

"Sure." Bill nodded. "Not much to report here. The doctor said it can be a slow, drawn-out process, so I guess we just have to be patient."

"I'm so sorry." He didn't know what else to say. He popped open the can and took a swig.

"I appreciate that. I'll be glad when this is over. But Emma's handling it really well tonight." He hooked a thumb over his shoulder in the direction of the ICU. "She's talking to her mom as if Caroline can hear her. No response, but Emma's not letting that stop her."

"Good for her."

Bill heaved a deep sigh and said again, "I'll be glad when this is over."

Tadhg only hoped when it was over, Caroline was able to be back home with her husband because she had completely recovered. He still hadn't seen her for himself, but from what Emma told him, it seemed pretty dire. And he knew that strokes could be devastating even if one survived.

Bill sank into the seat across from Tadhg and motioned for him to sit too. "While Emma's with her mom, I wanted to talk to you about something."

"Sure..." Tadhg waited.

"I think we need to tell Emma about her...story. I don't know if Caroline will ever be able to do it herself, and after she struggled with the decision for so long, she was finally firm in wanting Emma to know the truth. Personally, I think she *needs* to know. And—" He hesitated for a few seconds. "There's probably another reason to tell her now."

"Oh?" His curiosity was piqued, but he didn't want to press.

"Some things that this whole situation"—he circled a hand to encompass the hospital—"has uncovered."

Tadhg shook his head. "That doesn't sound good."

"I'll explain everything. It's just for future precaution. But I do think she should know."

"Okay. I think it would help her a lot—to know. Not just to learn the truth about her birth parents, but to know that her mom had decided to share the truth with her. That was the thing that really bothered her. That it was a barrier between them."

Bill nodded. "I agree. I think, too, that if Caroline does...come back to us...if she's aware, it might be a relief for her to know that Emma's already been told."

"That makes sense. So, what are you thinking? I mean, when do you want to talk to her?"

"As soon as possible. It's kind of weighing on *me*. It's a big responsibility. But I'd like you to be there when I do talk to her, Tadhg. She trusts you and feels safe with you. That's very clear when I see you two together." He hesitated a moment, then went on. "I honestly wondered if maybe I should tell you the details, and see what you think her reaction will be. In fact, the news might be better coming from you than from me. But—I hate to put that off on you."

That didn't really feel right. He didn't want to find out Emma's history one second before she did. There were already too many secrets. He deflected. "No, I'm happy to be there with her when you talk to her. I think she'll handle it okay."

"I'm glad you think so. I'm so sorry she's had to bear up under so much. Don't get me wrong, I admire Caroline's sense of honor to keep the promise she made. But those people are gone now, and Emma is an adult. There's no reason she shouldn't know."

"I agree with you. But one good thing: She's gotten stronger through all of this in just the short time I've known her."

"Good. Good... Well, let's figure out a time to meet. Get this over with. Do you want me to come to the island?"

Tadhg shook his head. "You probably don't want to travel that far from the hospital. We can come here."

"I appreciate that."

"I was planning to drive her over again tomorrow night. Would it work for us to come then? After she's seen her mom?"

"Assuming nothing changes with Caroline, yes." Bill brightened. "Maybe we can finally eat that birthday cake that's been sitting in the fridge for a week. Caroline had it all packed up to go in Tupperware, so it should still be good."

"That would be nice. Emma will like that." He floated an idea. "Listen, unless you'd rather I didn't, I think I should prepare her for what you're going to be telling her. She still doesn't know that I talked to you and Caroline that night. If—and I don't think she will—but if by some chance she decides she'd rather *not* know, are you okay with that?"

Again a long hesitation. "I think she needs to know now, Tadhg. For...medical reasons."

Now he was beyond curious. And more than a little concerned. But he would wait, the way Emma had.

They arranged a time to meet Bill at the house in Georgetown tomorrow night. Tadhg hated knowing what Emma faced when she was unaware. But he would warn her on the drive over tomorrow, and soon, they would both know the truth. And however hard that truth might prove to be, he thought—*prayed*—it would be healing for Emma.

July

A WEEK ago today she'd been celebrating her birthday, falling in love with Tadhg, slowly coming to terms with the truth of her life. So much could change in the blink of an eye.

Tadhg had insisted on driving her to the hospital tonight. Since Mom had begun to come out of sedation, they were tapering off her meds with each dose. Bill had told her it was hard to watch and warned her that Mom had been even more vocal than last night.

When she'd told Tadhg that and said he didn't have to come if he didn't want to, he'd surprised her. "No, I want to come. It's the only way I get to see you these days. And besides, Bill has invited us to his house—for birthday cake."

She laughed, remembering the way Tadhg had scrunched up his nose and asked, "Is birthday cake good after a whole week?"

She'd assured him it would be fine. "As long as it's been covered in the fridge, pound cake should still taste good. It might be a little dry. Maybe we could pick up some ice cream to take over. But I wouldn't miss it for the world. So, when did you talk to Bill?"

"Last night. In the waiting room. We had a good talk. And I wanted to tell you something before we get there."

She studied him. Something was up. "Okay..."

"You were supposed to find this out on your birthday, but with everything that happened, it just...seemed like it could wait. I just don't want you to think I was keeping secrets from you."

"What are you talking about, Tadhg?"

He told her then about going to Georgetown and talking to Mom and Bill. Inviting them to the party. "Please don't be angry with me. I just knew that having your mom there was probably the only gift you really wanted. And I had a feeling she was missing you as much as you were missing her."

"Oh, Tadhg. How could I be angry. So, Mom didn't argue? Bill didn't have to talk her into it?"

"No. Quite the opposite." He reached across to take her hand. "And Emma, before her...accident, your mom planned to answer your questions about your adoption."

"What?" Her cheeks grew warm. "How do you know that?"

"She told me. And Bill agreed that you should know."

A sob came suddenly. "Now I may never know."

He squeezed her hand. "No, Emma. You *will* know. Bill is going to tell us tonight."

"He...knows?"

Tadhg nodded.

"She kept the secret from me, but she told him?"

"Emma, please don't go there. Someday when *you* are married, I hope you won't ever keep a secret from...your husband."

She understood what he was saying and somewhere deep inside of herself, it struck a chord of joy within her. But she only gave him a soft nod. "Did they tell *you*?"

"No. No, of course not. Only that they planned to tell you. Your mom didn't want to tell you on your birthday in case it upset you. But she said soon. And then, of course, she couldn't. But Bill thinks you should know. And he feels that it will be a relief to your mom...once she comes out of this...to know that you've already been told."

She sat, stunned, in the passenger seat, clinging to Tadhg's hand. She was going to find out the truth. Tonight.

She felt his eyes on her, and he said softly. "Are you ready for this?"

"I don't know." She gave a humorless laugh. "Isn't that crazy. I've demanded to know, and now I'm not sure I want to."

"I think you should. Even if it's hard." He slipped his hand from hers and wiped his palm on his jeans. "I can wait in the car if you'd rather I not be there when you talk to Bill."

"No! I want you there. Please."

He took her hand again. "Then I'll be there."

They drove in silence for a while, but as they got closer to Savannah, she turned to him. "Is he going to tell me their names? My birth parents? And how they died?"

"I think whatever you want to know. At least however much Bill knows."

The moment she'd wanted so desperately was minutes away, and she honestly wasn't sure now how she felt about it.

Chapter Thirty

Bill lifted the Peach Caramel Pound Cake from the large Tupperware holder and set it on the kitchen counter. "There. That doesn't look too bad does it? For week-old cake, I mean?"

Tadhg laughed. "It looks pretty great, actually."

"Thanks for bringing the ice cream," Bill said. "That was a good call. I'll slice the cake if you'll dish up, Tadhg."

"Sure, happy to."

"And Emma, the caramel topping is in the fridge. Your mom bought a new bottle for the occasion. Oh, but wait!" Bill opened a drawer and brought out a package of birthday candles. "We'd planned to stop and get candles for your cake on our way to the island Tuesday. I'm sorry, but we've only got twenty here. We'll just have to pretend about the other eight."

"I'm fine with twenty." She watched these two men she loved work together to load the cake with candles and her heart swelled, even as she trembled with emotion at what was coming.

Bill lit the candles and Tadhg joked, "If we were worried about the cake drying out before, this ought to put it over the edge."

The candles flared and Bill laughed. "Sing! Quick!"

The two did a more than decent job with the birthday song, and Emma tried not to cry as she blew out the candles. If only Mom could be here with them.

Bill sliced cake and Tadhg scooped ice cream and drizzled the requisite caramel topping over each serving. They made small talk while they ate, but Emma sensed that all three of them were eager to get this conversation over with. When they'd finished eating, the two men cleared the table.

She protested. "I'm not helpless, you guys."

"We know. But it's your birthday." Tadhg planted a discreet kiss in her hair.

"Belated," she reminded them.

When Tadhg started to rinse the dishes, Bill waved him away. "I'll do those later. Let's sit down."

They joined her at the table and Bill dove in. "I guess Tadhg told you what I wanted to talk to you about tonight?"

She nodded, willing herself not to turn into a puddle of emotion.

Tadhg scooted his chair closer and reached for her hand under the table. She didn't know if she could ever love him more than she did in this moment.

"Emma, your mom really struggled with whether to tell you, but in the end, she was resolute that you should know. And I agree. This is going to be a little tough to wrap your head around, but the important thing to remember is that your mom and dad are true heroes. You might have had a very different life—" He swallowed hard and started again. "Things would have been very different if your mom and dad hadn't made the choice to adopt you. I don't want to just blurt this out, so let me tell you first that you actually knew your birth parents. You knew them quite well."

She shook her head. "I don't understand."

"About twenty-nine years ago, your grandparents—your Grandma and Grandpa Baker—found themselves in a really tough situation. Your grandma was forty-nine years old when she found out she was pregnant." Bill waited for the implications of his words to sink in.

And when they did, Emma gasped. "With me?" she whispered.

Bill nodded. "With you. Your grandpa was even older than her, and they just couldn't imagine raising a baby to adulthood at their age. I think your mom said your grandpa would have been over seventy when you graduated college. They didn't think it would be good for you, or for them, to try to raise you. But they also couldn't imagine putting you up for adoption and likely never seeing you again, maybe never even knowing what happened to you. So your mom came up with a plan. She and your dad were engaged at the time, and your dad was one hundred percent onboard."

It struck her then, like a bolt of lightning. "So Mom is actually...my sister?"

"She's your *mom*, honey. In every way that matters. She always will be. But yes, biologically, she's your sister."

"So was Grandpa...the father? *My* father? Or did something else...?" She couldn't let herself think about what might have happened.

But Bill nodded emphatically. "Oh, yes. Yes. It was nothing like that...no affair or...assault or anything inappropriate. No, your birth parents are your Grandma and Grandpa Baker. And your mom is your full biological sister. So, you see? You knew your birth parents growing up all along."

In all the possibilities she'd imagined, this one had never crossed her mind. But now the DNA test results made sense. Her DNA was that of Mom's parents, so it made sense that it had been much the same as Mom's.

And she had a sister. How often had she told people Mom was more like a sister and a friend? But in her mind, she couldn't separate those relationships—mom, sister, friend. Could they all exist in one person who she called Mom?

"I know it probably seems kind of strange, honey, but I hope it's also comforting to know that there's no unknown mom or dad out there that you never got to know. You knew and loved your birth parents and they loved you. More than you'll likely ever know on this side of heaven."

Tadhg squeezed her hand and looked at her with the same incredulous expression she knew her own face must wear right now.

She shook her head. "Wow. That's... I never in my wildest dreams would have guessed that...scenario."

Bill chuckled. "No, I suppose not. Your mom said it was kind of hard for all of them at first. Awkward, I guess is a better word. And for a while, your grandparents kind of backed away. It hurt her feelings at first, but Caroline thinks now that they did it so she and Tony—your dad—could establish their family without...well, without those rather complicated circumstances hanging over them. But I'm sure you have memories of how much they loved you and enjoyed you. Yes, things were kind of tense between them at first, but your mom said after a while, it was like nobody remembered the details that didn't matter. She told me that sometimes months would go by and she would barely even think about how you came to them. You were just *theirs*, plain and simple. And then she'd be a little shocked when something reminded her."

Emma nodded, trying to fit all the puzzle pieces into place in her mind. She felt grateful that it wasn't something that had consumed Mom, but right now she couldn't imagine it not consuming *her* for the rest of her life.

"And of course," Bill said, "It all became that much more of a gift and a blessing after your mom couldn't conceive. She was so grateful to her mom then, for allowing *her* to be a mother. I hope you can see what a really beautiful thing it is, Emma."

"But then... Why wouldn't they tell me?"

"Honey, that I don't know. I mean, for your mom, it was because she had promised your grandparents she wouldn't tell a soul. You have to understand that things were different back then.

Open adoption was still a new thing—or at least an unusual thing —and people were just a little more private about things like that than they are now. I'm purely speculating, but I would guess your grandparents were afraid some people would be judgmental about their decision."

She nodded, trying to put herself in Grandma's shoes. "And maybe she was afraid if I knew, I would be hurt by her decision to give me up. Maybe that's why she made Mom promise not to tell."

"That makes sense to me." Bill shrugged. "I suppose there are some things we'll never know. Things even your mom didn't know maybe. But please be comforted by the fact that Caroline— your mom—ultimately decided that her relationship with you was more important than a secret she'd felt trapped by for a lot of years."

Her mind was spinning. "I just can't wrap my head around this. I have so many questions."

"I know." Bill patted her hand on the table, and Tadhg squeezed her other hand underneath the table.

"It's a lot," Bill said. "As you have questions, I'll try to answer them—or better yet, Lord willing, your mom will be well enough and she can fill in the blanks. But in the meantime, honey, I hope you'll choose to see the beauty in it. Especially how precious it was for your mom and dad. What a gift you were to them. And for you, what a gift it was to be raised by two such fine people. Of course, I didn't know Tony, but Caroline has certainly painted a heroic picture of him. It sounds like he was a great dad."

"He was." She teared up, missing Dad in a way she hadn't in a long time. "Thank you, Bill. Thank you so much for telling me."

He cleared his throat. "There's one other thing I need to mention...it's one of the things that I think helped your mom decide about whether or not to tell you. She told you there was nothing serious in your medical background. Caroline had just been diagnosed with high blood pressure, but it was well controlled with her medication. She didn't think it was any big deal. But, obviously, after what happened last week, you'll want to talk to your doctor—not now, of course, but as you get older. And keep an eye out for any symptoms. Your mom's research said that high blood pressure *can* be hereditary, but not necessarily so... Just take that for what it's worth."

Emma nodded soberly.

"I hope you're not upset by what I've told you." Bill looked at her plaintively.

"No. I'm thankful. I really am. It's going to take a while for me to process everything, but at least I know now." They all sat quietly for a minute. And then a question came to her. "Do you know if Nonno and Nonni knew my story? Did they know I was adopted? And who my birth parents were?"

He nodded. "They were the only other ones who knew. Your dad insisted on that. He didn't want any secrets from his parents. And it didn't change a thing about how much they loved you. Caroline always said they were so proud that you carried the Fiori name."

She felt a huge gush of relief. Nonno and Nonni wouldn't have left the house to her if it had mattered to them that she wasn't their flesh and blood.

Bill rose from the table and she and Tadhg did the same. Tadhg put an arm around her and she let herself lean into his strength.

"Listen," Bill said, "I know you'd planned to go see your mom tonight, but why don't you take a break. I'll go see her and I'll text you later to let you know how she is. You two go do something fun. Or just go out to dinner." He grinned. "Since you've already had your dessert."

TADHG FELT SO happy and relieved for Emma. He could almost see the burden that had lifted from her shoulders. And if he was honest with himself, it lifted a weight from him, too. Even if it took a while for her to process everything, he felt sure a healing had begun in her tonight.

She said as much once they were seated in the restaurant. River House Seafood was on the waterfront in Savannah's historic district, and the atmosphere dockside on the riverwalk was festive and bright tonight. It was just what they needed, Tadhg thought. Although as he perused the menu, he was grateful Bill had slipped them a fifty-dollar bill before they left his house, insisting they use it to eat "somewhere nice."

He reached across the table and took her hand. "So, how are you doing?"

She nodded. "Okay. I think. It's all pretty...*wild*. Don't you think?"

"Honestly, Emma? It's surprising maybe, but I think it's really neat. A lot of the things you worried about—at least what you told me—are kind of answered now that you have the truth."

She tilted her head. "Like?"

"Like worrying that you never got to know your birth parents. And wondering what they were like, whether they loved you, and if so how could they give you up? And the health records thing. You got all those questions answered. And—" He shrugged. "It seems to me that everything worked out pretty well."

She gave him a crooked smile. "Romans 8:28."

"Exactly."

She was quiet for a minute, but when she looked up at him again, that gleam was in her eyes. The one he'd first seen that night in the garden when he'd taken her portrait. The one that said she loved him.

"Tadhg, I don't know how I ever would have gotten through this without you. Thank you."

"You are a strong woman, Emma Fiori. I have a feeling you would have gotten through just fine."

"But I'm so glad I didn't have to. You always knew just what to say. When to let me talk about it, but also when to do something to take my mind off of it."

He shrugged and cocked his head. "I'm nice that way."

"Yes, you are. You are *very* nice that way."

"Did I mention that I love you?"

"Once or twice, I think, but would you mention it again? Just for good measure."

She didn't think she'd ever forget the look on his face when he said it once again.

Chapter Thirty-One

"Why is it so dark in here, Mom?"

The answer was a slow, garbled mess that made no sense at all to Emma. Aphasia had to be the absolute worst injury a stroke bestowed on its victim. She crossed her mother's room and opened the curtains to reveal a deep, dusty windowsill and a drab view of the rehab center's parking lot. She made a note to bring some nice flowering plants with her next time she came to visit.

They'd moved her mom from the hospital to the rehab center a week ago, and Emma hoped there wouldn't be too many more visits here before Mom would be back home with Bill in Georgetown. But she was a little discouraged by how little change there'd been, despite hours of physical and speech therapy. It was even harder to come and see her here than it had been in the ICU—maybe because this was the last hope before a decision had to be made about whether Mom would ever be able to go back home to live or if she would need some sort of assisted living or nursing care plan for the rest of her life.

Not even sixty years old. Her mom didn't belong here. Even with the droopy, lopsided face the stroke had given her, Mom looked young enough to be the daughter of most of the residents here.

When she finished adjusting the curtains, she turned to see Mom waving her left hand, beckoning Emma to sit in the chair beside her. Her right arm rested impotently in her lap, propped on a bed pillow, and her right leg sported a boot and brace.

"How are you feeling today?" She put an arm around her mom and tried not to give in to the temptation to speak in a slow, mimicking drawl. The therapists had said to speak slowly and clearly but not to talk down to her or try to speak for her. That wasn't an easy assignment.

She went to the counter to retrieve the little bouquet of flowers she'd brought from the garden. She set them on the end table by Mom's chair.

Her eyes lit and she gave Emma a crooked smile.

"Aren't the strawflowers pretty this year?"

Mom gave a lopsided nod and Emma felt sure she'd understood the question.

Mom pressed her lips together. "Bill?"

Emma's eyes widened as the name rolled from her mom's lips, clear as a bell.

Mom's eyes twinkled as if she knew she'd said it correctly.

"Wow, Mom. That's great. The therapy must be helping, huh?"

Mom looked frustrated and said his name again, this time the question clear in her rising inflection.

"Oh, sorry. *How* is Bill? You can ask him yourself. He'll be here tonight like he always is."

Mom seemed to relax at that reminder. Then she sat forward again, working her mouth. "Em-ma?" It sounded more like *enema*, but Emma wasn't about to complain.

"You're doing so well, Mom." She beamed.

Mom beamed back, but then repeated Emma's name, more clearly this time, but with the same question in her inflection.

Emma giggled and patted her chest. "Oh, you mean how am I?"

That crooked nod again. She seemed delighted to be understood.

"I'm good, Mom. Really good." And getting better by the minute as she realized the improvement that had happened almost overnight. Maybe the sedatives they'd given Mom in the ICU were just finally getting out of her system, and the natural healing of time had taken hold. Whatever miracle God was doing here, it gave Emma more hope than she'd felt in the two weeks since the stroke.

She lifted the little vase of flowers. "The garden's going crazy, but that's good because I have two weddings this month and I'm trying to do the farmers market every weekend I don't have a wedding."

She struggled to keep a one-sided conversation going, but it was far easier than it had been last week, with Mom now nodding along and seeming to comprehend everything she said. "Oh, I almost forgot to tell you. Bill had Tadhg and me over to eat the birthday cake you made. Tadhg had his doubts, but it was still delicious even after a week."

"Hap-hap to you." Mom sang a little off key. But then, off key was normal for Mom.

"It was a hap-hap birthday. Really hap-hap. Thank you." She wondered if her mother realized that she'd had the stroke on Emma's birthday?

But Mom laughed, and it was her familiar, musical laugh. Emma laughed easily along with her, but inside, she was weeping for joy.

"Did Bill tell you," she risked, "that he told me—all about Grandma and Grandpa Baker?"

Mom nodded and her gaze pierced Emma.

"I know now, and everything is okay, Mom. I'm glad I know. It's going to be okay."

"Goo-ood. Good." Her left hand groped for Emma.

She reached across the table and took the warm hand in hers. It had been a long time since she'd seen her mom so content. Risking tears, she whispered, "Thank you, Mom. For raising me. And loving me."

"Yo... Dad..."

"Yes, Dad too. You guys did good. Just look how I turned out." She struck a *ta-dah* pose.

Mom chuckled at her joke. But then she couldn't seem to stop laughing. It was a phenomenon the rehab center had warned her about. Erratic emotions and uncontrollable laughter or tears.

Emma just kept laughing softly with her until she quieted. But then there were tears rolling down Mom's cheeks. She couldn't tell if this was part of the erratic emotions, but she thought they were genuine tears. She squeezed her mom's hand. "Are those happy tears or sad?"

The droopy face crumpled and then she blurted out, "Both."

"Yes." Emma nodded. "Me too." And she felt like she was getting her mother back.

They cried together a little then. And when they were done, they laughed some more. And it felt exactly right.

"Hey, sweetheart, how was your day?"

It was Bill. *Thank you, dear Lord, for this faithful man.*

His kiss gave no indication that he noticed her droopy smile or her crippled body.

"Did you have any visitors?"

She concentrated, wanting him to see how she was improving, how hard she was trying to get well for his sake. "Emma. Emma... came."

"Oh, that's wonderful, Caroline. I'm so glad."

She rehearsed the words in her mind before she opened her mouth. "She...told...me."

His eyes said he understood. "I'm glad. She took it well, sweet-

heart. I'm sure it took some getting used to, but she's strong. Every-thing will work out."

She nodded. She tried to frame the question she needed an answer to, but when she spoke, she could tell by his expression that it wasn't coming out right.

But then, as if he'd read her mind, he took her hand and bent to speak intimately. "She only knows what she needs to know. The rest will die with us."

The sigh she breathed out felt like she'd held it for decades. And indeed, she had. But that was all over now. The secrets that needed to be kept with God were safely in His hands. And those she should have shared long ago, had finally been revealed—and accepted with grace.

All she had to do now was work to get better so she could enjoy the rest of her life with the precious husband and daughter God had given her.

She reached for Bill with her good, strong hand and spoke clearly, with joy. "Thank you."

TADHG REFRESHED the browser on his laptop and checked his bank balance again. His first salaried payday was a pleasant surprise. His take-home pay more than made up for the overtime he'd been getting. Best of all, with the new hire taking up some slack, and another coming in September, he hadn't had to work much more than forty hours the last two weeks, which had allowed him time to do some thrifting.

Izzy had let him use a corner of her garage to refinish some small furniture pieces he'd found, and he was kind of getting into this woodworking thing. The tiny garage left a lot to be desired as a workshop, but it would do for now.

He signed out of his account and checked the time. Emma was making dinner for them tonight and he'd promised to stop by

Winn-Dixie for a certain parmesan cheese she needed for a garnish.

SHE GREETED him at the door wearing an apron.

"Ooh, this must be serious," he teased, kissing her cheek. "You look cute."

She ignored him and looked expectantly at his empty hands. "Did you forget my Parmigiano Reggiano?" She rolled her R's and leaned into her adopted Italian heritage. It was a good sign.

He pulled the wedge of cheese from the pocket of his cargo shorts, which earned him a smile.

Following her into the kitchen, he caught a whiff of something savory and amazing. "Mmm... I can't wait."

"Well, you'll have to. Just twenty minutes."

"I'll be patient. Did you see your mom today?"

"Oh, Tadhg. You wouldn't have believed it."

He stopped and studied her. "Why? What happened?"

She told him how her mom had spoken Bill's name clearly and even sang "Happy Birthday" to her when she told her about eating the peach cake she'd made.

"That's incredible. Maybe she *will* come back from this completely." To be honest, he'd had his doubts given Emma's reports up till now.

"Oh, I pray she will, Tadhg." She gave a little chuckle. "But I'm prepared for it to be a slow process. I saw Bill in the parking lot when I was leaving, and when I told him, he confessed that Mom had called him 'Tony' just as clearly yesterday. Twice."

"Oh, ouch." He winced.

But Emma shrugged. "Bill's a good sport. He said he wasn't going to complain, given how he knew Mom felt about my dad. And how clearly she was speaking."

"That's a good man."

She nodded. "I have a whole new appreciation for that man.

Not that I didn't like him before, but he has been a prince to Mom through all this."

"He's a good man," he said again. *Someone to emulate.* "Hey, speaking of princes, you never mentioned what you thought of my birthday card."

"Your card?" She wrinkled her freckled nose. "I haven't even gotten you one yet. Your birthday isn't till September, right?"

"No, silly, the card I gave *you*. It was in a big purple envelope. I put it on the table with all the birthday decorations." He pointed to the windows where he'd set up the folding table the night of her birthday.

She shook her head. "I don't remember that. Are you sure it made it here?"

"I'm positive. It was leaning up against those windows behind the package that had your necklace in it."

She had opened the dainty silver cross necklace the night of her birthday after they got back from the ICU, and she'd worn it constantly ever since.

"A purple envelope? I don't see how I could miss that."

"Not dark purple. More...lavender, I guess. Or violet? I don't know my colors."

"Oh, lavender. I do remember. Oh, Tadhg, I hope it didn't get thrown away. The trash went out the day after my party. What was in it?"

"Nothing I can't replace. But I did spend hours writing a very sweet note to you."

"Hours?" She looked dubious.

"Well, minutes anyway."

Looking chagrined, she walked over to the windows and pulled the curtains back, first on the left side, then the right. "Oh, look. There it is. It must have fallen behind here when you cleaned off the table that night." She shook the hem of the curtain before letting it fall. "Wow, somebody needs to vacuum in here."

"So, open it."

She looked at him, curiosity in her gaze. He couldn't even

remember exactly what he'd written, but he remembered the important part.

She opened the envelope and slipped out the card. Two slips of paper fell from it. "Oh, what's this?" She caught one of them before it hit the floor. She read his hand-printed certificate aloud: "'Good for one trip to the top of the Saint Simons Island Lighthouse.' Oh, that's perfect, Tadhg. I love it."

"Wait though…" He bent to rescue the second slip of paper from the floor and handed it to her with a grin. "This is the good one."

She read it: "'Good for one kiss at the top of the Saint Simons Island Lighthouse.'" She rushed him and wrapped her arms around his neck reaching for a kiss.

"Huh-uh…" He held her back, teasing. "You have to wait to collect at the top of the lighthouse."

She giggled. "Then we'd best go tomorrow because I'm not waiting much longer for permission to kiss you."

He touched his lips lightly to hers. "Okay, maybe just a little one to tide you over. I don't think I can get away for a couple of weeks, and we might want to wait until the weather cools down a little."

"That'll be September."

"How about we go on my birthday? The 10th?"

"It's a date. But why can't you get away for a couple of weeks?"

He smiled. "My brothers are coming to visit next week. Both of them, with their families."

"Oh, that's wonderful."

"Apparently Liam and Kacey had such a good time here they convinced Declan's crew to come back with them. I want you to meet them."

"Of course. I can't wait."

"And then I want to take you to Ohio to meet Mom and Dad. Do you think you could get away for five or six days to drive to Ohio? Early September?"

"I can't wait to meet your parents, but I have book club here the seventh. Can we wait until after that? I think I can get the garden put to bed by the middle of the month. Or I can just let it go wild and deal with it when we get back."

"I'll help you with the garden when we get back—whatever you need me to do."

For the rest of my life.

Chapter Thirty-Two

September

Emma shaded her eyes and looked through the trees to where the lighthouse towered above them. Beside her, Tadhg did the same. He'd turned thirty at 8:07 this morning, according to his mother. They'd talked to her together this morning, and Emma couldn't wait to meet her and Tadhg's dad in Ohio at the end of the month.

"It looks like there's a storm brewing."

"I told you there's rain in the forecast. But not till noon."

"Well, we'd better get going then." He put a hand at the small of her back and guided her forward. "I want to be first in line when they open."

There were a few people milling about the grounds, but the museum was empty inside, and there was no queue at the gift shop where tickets were sold.

"Are you ready for this? It's 129 steps, you know."

She scoffed. "That's nothing compared to the steps I walk in the garden every day."

"Maybe, but up and down a winding staircase is different."

She flexed her muscles. "I know. I'm ready."

He paid for the tickets, and the docent led them to the door of the stairwell. "You pretty much have the place to yourselves," the woman said. "I think the forecasted storms scared people off."

"We're not afraid of a little storm, are we?" Tadhg looked to Emma to back him up.

But she read the subtext in his comment, too. "No, we are not afraid." She smiled up at him.

But the docent turned stern. "That's all well and good, but if there's lightning or if the wind comes up any more, the museum will close. So if the weather gets at all iffy while you're in the tower, you need to come down immediately."

"Yes, ma'am, we will." He nodded solemnly.

Hearing his bravado turn to meekness, Emma hid a smile behind her hand.

The door closed behind the docent, leaving them in the tower alone. He held his arm wide. "After you?"

"You'll catch me if I fall?" Their voices echoed in the narrow chamber.

"I'll do my best. But don't think I'm going to carry you if you can't make it to the top."

She took his implicit dare and raced up the circular stairway. But by the time they got to the second landing with a lookout, she was breathing hard.

"Huffing and puffing a little, are you?"

"Hush, old man." She went to the open window to peer out.

He came and stood behind her, wrapping her in his arms and resting his chin on the top of her head. The view was mostly rooftops and trees from here. Emma ducked around him and hurried up the next flight.

"You're gonna kill me, woman," he called out from below.

She peered over the rail and waved at him from two flights above. "If you weren't so old, maybe you could catch me." She was winded, but she wasn't about to let him see that.

But he caught up with her at the next landing and captured her in his arms. She leaned back against his chest, and they watched out the window as a bank of dark clouds rolled in.

She frowned. "I hope that lady isn't going to make us come down."

"Then we'd better hurry to the top before she stops us."

He beat her to the next section of stairway, and she had to scamper to keep up with him. She reached the top one second after him, and together they stepped out onto the observation deck just below the lantern gallery surrounding the lighthouse.

Breathing hard, they stared out across the sea, then turned to look at each other in awe. The view from this perspective would have been stunning on any ordinary day, but the storm rolling in made it truly breathtaking. The scent of the sea wafted up to them and the ocean breeze became a squall and blew their hair in every direction. They laughed as they tried to balance against the wind, Tadhg hanging on to the rail with his right hand and hanging on to her with his left. They made their way around seaside where there was a little protection from the wind and stopped again to gaze out over the waves.

In the distance the grasses in the salt marshes undulated in the wind, and the storm clouds built and billowed. Watching the waters churn beneath them, it struck her as a perfect metaphor for what she'd been through these past four months. She tried to express what she was feeling to Tadhg. "It's like the storm surrounded me. Above"—she pointed to the roiling clouds and then the thrashing waves—"and below. Sometimes it seemed like there was no escape."

He smiled down at her and brushed a strand of hair from her forehead. "And yet, here we are, standing on the precipice but safe and out of reach of either the clouds or the waves."

"So true." Her breath caught. "God was here all along. Even when I couldn't feel it. And it was Him who controlled it all—the waves and the wind..."

He pulled her closer. "Sometimes I think He has to stir up the sea of our lives a little just to get our attention. Or to move us in a different direction."

She nodded against him, knowing he was right. Tipping her head back, she gazed up at him. "I kind of like the direction He's been moving me."

"As long as it's in *my* direction, I do too."

"Happy birthday, Tadhg," she whispered.

"It's already been a good one."

"I can't wait for you to open your present." She'd conspired with his brothers and found an antique tool he told Liam he'd been wanting for a certain woodworking project. She would give it to him at dinner tonight. He'd been doing some beautiful furniture restorations, and she secretly hoped that a few of those pieces might end up in her house someday...when it was *their* house.

He nuzzled her hair. "I already gave myself the best present ever."

"Oh? What's that?"

"This day with you."

"Wait a minute..." She looked up at him and narrowed her eyes. "So, you're telling me that when you gave me those gift certificates to go up in the lighthouse for *my* birthday, they were really for *your* birthday?"

He had the decency to look sheepish. "To be fair, I didn't know it at the time. But come to think of it, we could save a lot of money in the future if we give gifts that way."

She gave him an elbow to the ribs. "*That's* what I think of that idea."

But the truth was, if they could live the rest of their lives with this realization—that they were each God's gift to the other—how rich their life together would be.

"But don't you want to collect on your other gift certificate?"

"That depends on if it's my birthday gift or yours." She eyed him coyly. "The certificate was for a kiss at the top of the lighthouse, as I recall."

"How about one for each of us?"

She turned into his embrace and lifted her face to meet his.

"How about two for each?"

"Deal."

And then he paid up, soft and sweet.

Epilogue

One year later

Emma took her iced coffee to the loggia, soaking in the last moments of summer. Already, the tall trees that bordered her property wore a haze of gold. The ancient moss-draped live oak that sheltered the house swayed in the breeze. When she was a kid, she'd loved to scale that tree. If she clambered high enough in its branches, she could just see across the salt marshes to the ocean in the distance. It had been a long time since she'd made that climb, but that day—a year ago now—when she and Tadhg had climbed to the top of the lighthouse, she'd felt the same sense of awe.

It seemed like a dream that now, the sense of awe was for what God was doing in her life. She finished her coffee and went inside for a last-minute walk-through. Everything was ready for book club tonight and Tadhg would be here to help her in a few minutes.

As if her thoughts had summoned him, she heard his truck coming up the driveway. She couldn't wait until that sound was the music of every evening of her life.

"Hey, love." He poked his head in the door "Are you ready for me?"

She went to greet him with a kiss. "Always."

"Do you need me to do anything?"

"No, I'm good. You're sure you remember how to do the ribbons?" She pointed to the table where all the flowers were cut and waiting in buckets.

"Don't worry your pretty little head. I've got this."

"Okay. They'll be here soon. Do you need something to eat first?"

"I grabbed a burger on the way home."

"Okay. There'll be good desserts when we're done. Oh! That's the doorbell." Emma took him by the shoulders and escorted him out the door that led to the side garden. She grabbed a can of Coke from the fridge and thrust it in his hands.

Bud appeared from the pantry and she scooted him out behind Tadhg. "Here. Bud can keep you company. Now, remember, once you hear the buzz calm down, you can come back in the kitchen and listen for your cue."

He rolled his eyes. "From what I hear, the buzz *never* calms down with this book club."

She kissed him, gave him a gentle shove, and hurried to answer the door, butterflies dancing in her belly.

Mindy and Julia came up the walk bearing desserts.

"Hey girls! Welcome." She hugged Mindy over the fancy cake carrier she held. "You can just put that on the table—unless it needs to go in the fridge."

"No, it's sliced and ready to serve. The house looks gorgeous as always."

"I'll just put these on the table." Julia held up a bag of cookies and made a beeline for the flower table. This was their second annual flower arranging book club. They'd read *A Year of Flowers* by Suzanne Woods Fisher this month. The collection of novellas had everyone in the mood to create bouquets for their own homes.

Last September's book club in the garden had been so popular that the women had requested to make it an annual event. Last fall, the garden had been so prolific, and so late, that the women had been able to cut their own blooms, but things were pretty much done blooming this summer. Still, with plenty of greenery to fill in, she'd managed to find enough blossoms for each member to make a little nosegay bouquet to take home.

Ten minutes later, all but two of the book club members were gathered around card tables, and after a brief business meeting, Mindy welcomed everyone and introduced Emma.

"Most of you were here last year, so you know that I'm a flower farmer"—she gave a little curtsy—"otherwise known as a gardener." She kept it short and sweet before explaining what they would be making tonight.

"Last year we did flower arrangements in vases you brought, but this year I thought we'd do something a little different, especially since things were pretty much done blooming yesterday. Anyway, I brought someone special in to demonstrate the ribbon wrap we'll be using for our nosegays tonight."

She pulled a sample bouquet from a little vase. "These are similar to what I make for bridesmaid bouquets." She glanced from face to face, wondering if anyone was catching on.

That was Tadhg's cue. He ducked into the room from the kitchen where he'd been laying low. "Now?"

She laughed and reached for his hand, pulling him closer. "Now."

Several of the members who'd met him waved and called out, "Hey, Tadhg. Welcome."

He looked charmingly shy and a little embarrassed by all the attention, and she couldn't have loved him more for it.

She held up the sample. "Friends, I know some of you already know this man, but I'd like to introduce..." She cleared her throat and paused for effect. "My *fiancé*..." She dragged out the word. "...Tadhg McKay."

The room erupted in gasps and cheers and dozens of breathless questions.

"What?" Mindy exploded. "How long have you been keeping this secret?"

Emma beamed. "Well, we've been discussing for a while, but Tadhg officially proposed last Friday. At the top of the lighthouse. On his birthday."

"Yeah..." He pulled her into a possessive side hug, obviously warming to the attention. "I figured what better gift to give myself than a wife." He shot her a knowing look. Oh, how she loved that all their secrets now were good secrets, sweet ones they shared only with each other.

The women laughed and whispered to each other as they eagerly gathered around the table. As she demonstrated how to arrange the flowers and greenery and bind the bouquet with floral tape, Emma told the story of how Tadhg had come to her rescue the night her wedding flowers froze. He did her proud, adding comedic notes to her story, then helping them wrap and pin the wide ribbon around their nosegays.

When it was time for the book discussion part, though, Tadhg bowed out. While the women filled their plates and carried them out to the loggia with their drinks, Emma fixed an overflowing plate for Tadhg and snuck it back to the kitchen to him. "Your reward," she whispered. "You were great, babe! They loved you."

He took the plate in one hand. "Not as great as you."

"Let's not argue."

He laughed. "Okay. I'll be too busy eating anyway."

"Okay. I need to run." She tiptoed to kiss him. "We're still on for tomorrow night, right?"

He stared at her, then captured her in his arms. "Emma June," he whispered, "We are still on for the rest of our lives."

My love for Saint Simons Island began when I was just a young woman living in landlocked Kansas and reading the novels of an author named Eugenia Price. Price made her island setting come to life, and even though I'd never been to Georgia or laid eyes on an ocean, I knew that someday I wanted to visit Saint Simons.

Little did I know that I'd be in my sixties before I finally set foot on the island, but it was every bit as wonderful as I'd always dreamed. And from that moment forward, I knew I wanted to someday set a novel there myself.

Fast forward to this past spring, and my husband, knowing I'd begun work on the book—and despite a very busy work and travel schedule—planned a research trip to Saint Simons and Jekyll Islands. Not only did we have a wonderful time—a true vacation—but I found the inspiration I'd been looking for to make *Who Stirs Up the Sea* come to life.

After returning home, a more interesting bit of research began. Like Emma, I took a DNA test "just for fun." Yes, it was for research for this novel, of course, but since I already know my family history on both sides, I didn't expect to find anything shocking, and I didn't—unlike Emma.

I've always taken pride in my family history. A watershed

moment in my life happened two years ago when we made our first overseas trip and I was privileged to stand in front of the home in York, England where my great-grandfather lived at the time his parents moved their family to America. Even though my DNA test didn't turn up any surprises, I've begun to discover, as Emma did, that while our ancestry might be interesting and even central to who we've become, the only "ancestry" that really matters is that we are God's children, adopted into His family, and made His own by the blood of Christ.

But to all who did receive him, who believed in his name,
he gave the right to become children of God, who were born,
not of blood nor of the will of the flesh nor of the will of man,
but of God.

John 1:12-13

That is the "DNA" I treasure, and I'm filled with gratitude that because Jesus willingly carried my sin and bore it on the cross, my name is written in the Book of Life. I hope you enjoyed *Who Stirs Up the Sea,* and I pray that you, too, know Him personally so that *your* inheritance is your name, written in that Book of Life.

See what great love the Father has lavished on us,
that we should be called children of God!
And that is what we are!

1 John 3:1
New International Version

DEBORAH RANEY's first novel, *A Vow to Cherish*, inspired the World Wide Pictures film of the same title and launched Deb's writing career. Forty-plus books later, she is a three-time Christy Award finalist, and her novels have won the ACFW Carol Award, Selah Award, RITA® Award, Foreword Indie Gold, and many others. Deb teaches at writers conferences across the country and served on the executive board of the 2500-member American Christian Fiction Writers organization for almost 18 years. With her husband, Ken Raney, she is a transplant to Southeast Missouri from their native Kansas. A few of her favorite things are: coffee mugs, rainy days, screened porches, empty journals, e-biking, Friday garage sale dates with her husband, houseplants in pretty pots, kaleidoscopes, memories of Paris, guacamole, colored pencils, and her fourteen grandkids in any combination (but especially one-on-one).

To keep up with Deb's latest news or to sign up for her email newsletter, visit: www.DeborahRaney.com

FOLLOW DEB ON SOCIAL MEDIA

@deborah.raney   @deborahraney   @authordebraney

For other books
by Deborah Raney

To learn more, visit:
deborahraney.com

www.ingramcontent.com/pod-product-compliance
Lightning Source LLC
Chambersburg PA
CBHW070500300726
48975CB00007B/2260